College Hill

COMMON SIMILARITIES
LEAD TO FRIENDSHIPS
AND RELATIONSHIPS

C. Z. KING

CZK Enterprise INC

Paperback ISBN: 978-1-73347-821-2
Hardback ISBN: 978-1-73347-820-5

Cover Photo © 2021 www.gettyimages.com.. All rights reserved - used with permission.

CZK Enterprise INC

PRINTED IN THE UNITED STATES OF AMERICA

TABLE OF CONTENTS

DEDICATION

This book is for everyone. This includes gay, straight, bi-sexual, lesbian, transgender/transsexual, married, single, Black, White, Hispanic, Asian, Latin and Jew. This book is for all of those who are looking for love in the right place and time. This book is for those who are looking to grow their lives and who are proud of what they found. This book is an inspirational, motivational, love story that has nothing but upward mobility.

Those that are looking for love will find strong love inside this book. Those who desire to pull yourself up by your bootstraps will find a path in this book. You will find strength and inspiration that will inspire you on your pathway to true happiness.

Acknowledgments

I would like to thank everyone who has been a part of my life. Without any of you, there would be no me. You all have contributed toward my life experience and have made me a better person. I would like to thank all of my classmates, friends and associates. I have learned a lot from all of you, and I hope when you read this book, you know it is coming from my heart. This book is all about love, and I am sure there is something relative to you all.

I was born in Mobile, Alabama. I was the first born to Mary Elizabeth King and Johnny White.

I would like to give special thanks to my husband/spouse, Donald J. Haywood. I love you, and I would never forget our wedding day in Washington, DC, October 25, 2013. Yes, it is legal, and we got papers. I would like to thank my family, my mother, father, brothers and sisters and all of my nieces and nephews. I would like to thank all of my aunts, uncles and cousins and my daughter, son-in-law and grandkids for being so supportive of me in my time of need.

*I am giving a special shout-out to my grandmother, Mary J. King, who has been a major inspiration in my life. She has shaped my thinking and sense of being that make me the person I am today. I do not know if I could have made it this far without her. **I LOVE YOU, MA. MAY YOU REST IN PEACE AND KNOW THERE IS NOT***

A DAY THAT GOES BY WITHOUT ME THINKING ABOUT YOU.

I have not forgot about you, "Bay" Eliza King; you are more than a second mother to me. I want you to know what you mean to me. I have never forgotten about you. I am still distraught that I could not get to see you when you passed when I was in France. **I LOVE YOU, AND I HOPE YOU ARE RESTING IN PEACE!!!!!**

Chapter 1

In the Beginning

Topeka, Kansas, has historical meanings to its existence, and they are not good. The city is known as the place that did not believe in segregation and the fairness of all ethnicities. Topeka is the place where it was known nationally that Blacks and Whites would not be in the same class. This was a clear violation of the law, and they were not going to get away with this. Thurgood Marshall took up the case of Oliver Brown. Mr. Brown sued for the rights of his daughter to be educated like any kid in America. He did not believe that his daughter should have less of an education because she was Black. When Mr. Brown's daughter was denied access to the school, this is when the situation went national. Thurgood Marshall came in, took the case and argued it before the Supreme Court in 1952; it became known as Brown v. Board of Education. When he won the case, the case sent shockwaves throughout the country. White people could not believe the court ruled in Marshall's favor. Well, what they did not realize is the fact of what the implications would be on the country for the rest of their lives. With Marshall winning this case was a combination of four other cases that were all combined into one. The impact of this case led to what many believe to be the Civil Rights Act, the Montgomery Boycott and the Voters Rights Act. This led to Marshall getting an appointment on the Supreme Court and becoming the first African American appointment in the history of the country. As a result, White people were protesting that they did not believe that their children should be educated with Black kids because their kids were smarter. This led to colleges and universities not being segregated without riots and fights. Overall, Topeka, Kansas, had a stain it could not remove. There were plenty of people who believed they were right. This led to most of Kansas desegregating and having a really negative impact on the Black citizens of the state. The kids were not educated the same, and it was figured that they would make a lasting impact on the lives of Black people that would take centuries to make right. Little did they know that there was a generation coming that would make an impact on Kansas that the world would take notice to.

My life has turned out to be better than I could have expected after the opportunities and decisions I have made. I have managed to graduate with a master's degree in accounting from Kansas University, and I have taken my CPA exam for Kansas, Michigan and California. These are the places that I want to have offices over time. Yes, I am going to start my own CPA firm and make it better than any firm in the country. I have managed to rope the man of my dreams whom I will love for the rest of my life. Right now, this experience has made me not only a better man but a better person. I am now able to see people for who they are and what they are. I have learned to not be so judgmental. I am able to love people for who they really are. My decision-making has changed to where I am so sharp now. If you are not careful, you will get cut. I have decided to open my first location in Kansas or California, but I will talk with Anthony to see how he feels about this. Who knows—I might be able to expand quicker than I thought. I liked to always remain positive and upbeat because I believe in me, and so does Anthony. I really believe that I am going set a new standard for small businesses. I am going to compete with the best of them and make a difference.

It was June 7, 1992, when Anthony and I moved to San

Diego to start our lives on our own. I passed my CPA exam in March of 1992, and we were thinking of moving on our own to create our own legacy. Before I took the exam, we were lying around and pondering if we were going to leave Kansas. We both came up with several reasons for us to stay here and live. I remember the Saturday morning before the exam, I woke up, we ate breakfast and we discussed what our lives would look like in Topeka. I said, "Anthony, I love you, and I know you love me, but I am sure our lives would be so much better if we were thousands of miles away from here. There is no way we can create our legacy by being here. I think we should move out to California, and we can establish everything we need and want. We will not have the influence of family or friends that will cause problems. What you think, baby—should we try California?" "Yes, baby, I think we can make it on our own. I am sure we will struggle for a bit, but we can make it. I know you are very independent, but I will have to be the bread winner initially. Remember, I love you, and I am not trying to overshadow you and make you feel less than favored. I want you to understand and agree because you know how yo ass get. You start fussing and cussing and slamming shit. It scares me, but you know I love you." "You are my man, my husband, so I want you to know I will cut a bitch. I am a jealous queen at times, and I will not share what is mine." "It's cool, baby, and I will support you like I want you to support me. My question to you is how are we going to break this to our families?" "Leave that to me, but I am going to need you to find a way to coax your mother to come to my parents' house so we can break the news." I called my parents and told them that Anthony and I needed to meet with them, and we asked his mother to come over because we needed to find out our genealogy. My mother was like "What? Kevin, what are you talking about?" I said, "Ma, why are you minimizing the way I am feeling?" She looked at me and laughed and then said, "Stop being so dramatic." Anthony's mother came over, and I said, "I am so grateful that you all are here. We asked you all here to tell you that we are moving to San Diego." They were all shocked and looking like we died. Everyone had a question at the same time, but I heard this from all: "How do you all expect to survive"? I said, "We are going to work and make our own legacy. Remember, I just passed my CPA exam, so I will be doing accounting instantaneously, and Anthony is going to do construction work. Guys, we are going to make our legacy. This is what your parenting has done, and we need to try to make it on our own. We know we will struggle a little, but we will be fine. We are married, so you all do not have to watch over us like schoolgirls. I promise you we will make it."

That day came, and we were on the road. Our parents were crying and wondering what the hell we were doing. I convinced them that we would make it, but we were going to California from Kansas. OMG!! That is a big difference. I started to have doubts, but I never expressed them. I was scared, but I knew one thing: my baby believed in me, and I knew he loved me. Reality started to set in, and I was thinking, "We are going to a real state with real cities. This will be nothing like Kansas." We packed the car with our belongings, and I asked my parents if we could leave the really heavy stuff there until we got settled. They said yes, and we were all packed by that time. When we got in the car, I looked at Anthony and said to him, "Baby you know how much I love you, but I want you to promise me that you will always love me and never leave me." "I promise, baby, and you know that I will protect you from anybody and anything. We are going to do this." We knew this drive would take three days, and we were doing this together, which was what made this so special. I set up a budget on an Excel spreadsheet. We sold Anthony's car because it was of no use to us, and we saved money from school and work. We had $10,000. We decided that we would stay in an extended stay hotel for a few weeks until we got work, and then we would look for a place. We knew that when we decided on San Diego that we both wanted to be in luxury and in a place that would keep us stress free. We wanted to make sure we would be on the beach. The budget had our money allocated down to the penny. We both felt confident that we would have work within a week and be in our place in two weeks.

We arrived in San Diego and were starstruck at the views riding into the city. We went to the In-Town Suites and paid for the first week. I was off by $50 of the budget because it cost us $1,000 for the week. We got something to eat and just lay in bed, watched TV and went to sleep. Reality set in for both of us that we were grown, and we must make our own way. We looked in each other's eyes and could see the concerned looks. My baby said to me, "Baby, we are going to be fine. We are going to get some sleep, get up in the morning and start looking for work. I want you to stop looking concerned and worried because we got each other and your big brain." We laughed. He said, "I know you are a little worried, but I feel confident that with your brains, we will start balling soon. Shit, you are the smart one, and I need you to keep me straight. Just know, your plans always work, and I am comfortable with that. You are the brains, and I am the brawn. Let's do this shit. We cool?" "Yes, baby, therefore, I love you so much. I always feel secure with you. That motivates me more than you will ever imagine." We got up and started our journey toward the rest of our lives. We ate breakfast and started by looking for work on our phones. We looked all day, and I got a few leads, but Anthony found a construction company that was hiring on the spot. He called them on the phone and got the chance to speak with both the foreman and the owner. He met them in person the next day and was hired. My baby was hired doing heavy equipment operating (backhoe/crane). I was so proud of him because he was on track already to be a supervisor/foreman. When he got home, he told me, "We are going out to celebrate." We splurged a little, and he told me, "Baby, I hope you are not feeling down, but I am so happy to take care of you. You deserve it, and I feel so much better doing it. You have always done it for me, this includes you helping me change my mentality. I am the man I am becoming because of you." Again, I felt so happy and secure because I knew I got a good man. What really made this better was the next week I got a job at one of the top CPA firms in San Diego. I was happy about it and decided that it was not a problem working for someone else at this point, but I knew this was not going to be forever. We moved into a nice, small apartment. I called my mom and told her of our progress and asked if she and dad could have some movers bring our stuff. She said, "Yes, baby," and we had our stuff in three days. We were on our way to being a real married couple doing married things.

Now that we are both working and making decent salaries, we opened a joint bank account, and I was teaching my baby about finance and money. We were saving money and living frugally. We were not going to get stuck in anyway. We were determined to succeed and prove to ourselves that we belonged. After living in this apartment for six months, I sat Anthony down and started a conversation about buying a house. I said, "Baby, we have been here half the time of this lease, but I think we should think about buying a house. All real estate in California is prime and worth the investment. I have done some numbers, and with both of us, we can get a house, and our credit makes it even better. I am thinking that we get this house." The house I showed Anthony raised his eyebrows; he said, "Are you sure we can afford that?" I said to him, "Yes, and this is how." The house was going for $300,000, but it had a lot of upside. I came up with our payments being $3,000 a month, and I budgeted with us adding more to our savings these last six months. He said, "OK, if you think we can do it, then I am fine with it. You are controlling the finances, and this is your area." We went to a realtor, and of course I did all the talking. I explained our situation and that we wanted this house when our lease was up. She did a prequalification and ran our credit. She said, "This house is right at your limit, but if you all want to, I can help you get out of the lease and into the house." We asked if we could have a couple of days and get back to her, and she said yes. We talked about this the whole day and decided that we wanted to proceed with getting the house. I called her and told her that we wanted the house. After that I spoke with Anthony about what this meant, including us putting $5,000 down. He understood and said, "It's fine, baby; I trust you. You are handling that." Everything was approved, and we were out of the lease at the end of the month and into our new house. We were building and moving up, but what was better was we were doing it together. We were creating a new chapter in our life. Thank you, Lord, for blessing us and helping us in our dreams.

Our house was a beautiful but typical floral yellow. We had a five-bedroom house that had a nice-size foyer that we decorated with nice art on both sides of the room. On the wall to the left was a black-and-white picture of Malcolm X while he was speaking and to the right was a large picture of Langston Hughes with his usual big, bright smile. It led to the staircase that looked like a scene from *Gone with the Wind*. The staircase was like a walk up to heaven. The poles along the staircase just had that old, traditional Southern look. The character was something that most look for when looking for a house you know you are going to keep. The staircase reminded me of Scarlett O'Hara. To the left of the staircase was the kitchen that was huge like I liked because I loved to cook. The appliances were stainless, including the stove that sat in the island right in the middle of the floor. To the right of the stairs were our offices; my office was the larger of the two. My office was bigger than Anthony's because I had more work to do than he did. We also had a pool that we loved to get in on those hot nights. We both loved to swim in the nude. Most of the homes in our community had pools, which was common there in San Diego. The weather was nice, and the warm nights made it a must-have. We used our pool all the time. Growing up, I never had a pool or access to one. It was the same for Anthony, so we took advantage of this one.

I called my parents and Anthony's mom on three-way, and we told them the news. They were very happy but were wondering how we could afford a house. I explained the process to them, and they were like "I do not understand that number stuff, but if you all are doing well, we are OK with it." We set goals for months and years in advance as to how we were going to upgrade the house and make it better. My baby was in construction, so this made it much easier to do the work. Our lives were growing and changing into the best things we could have ever imagined. Anthony was starting to do plans for the expansion of the house and improvements to die for. We laughed and joked about our parents, but I noticed that Anthony was not happy that his father was not on the call. He never told me the whole story as to how he left and what happened, but you could see he was missing his father. We were going to have to do something about that.

Chapter 2

The Invitation

My alarm clock went off at 6:00 a.m., but I was already up. I hit the off button and slowly got out of bed, careful not to wake Anthony. He was a deep sleeper, and nothing could wake him. I was excited about getting out of the house this morning. As I went into the kitchen to make a pot of coffee, I looked out the window and could see the sun coming up. I turned on the TV to CNN and saw that the weather today was going to be 84 degrees on this Sunday. A typical day in Southern California. I loved the weather here in San Diego. The weather was perfect. I put on a pot of coffee and then headed to the bathroom to take a shower. Today was my day. A day that was going to be a chill day at the beach. I needed this "me" day. Anthony understood how much I loved to go to the beach and watch the water hit the shore and to enjoy the sun on my body. He liked the ocean as well, but he also knew I loved it more and would spend more time there then he would want to.

After I got out the shower, I looked in on him, and he was still knocked out. He was naked as always. He hated sleeping in anything. He always just slept with no clothes on, just totally nude. I told him that I get cold at night, but he always said to me that I needed to sleep closer to his hot body. He always said his body was the best heater in the world. As always, he was right. He was in a deep sleep and snoring. I wondered what he was dreaming about. I just knew he was dreaming of me. I loved this man with all of my being. If I was not going to the beach, I might have to wake him with the morning special. He loved the special and was always on deck and ready to serve me. The ocean was calling me, and I couldn't wait to watch the waves crashing against the shore. I thought I was going to wake him and give him the special because I knew it was what he wanted.

We had just had a long and passionate lovemaking session. He held me so close and tightly as though I were going to leave. I felt so comfortable the way he held me. He took his time and proved that he loved me while making love. His love sent me into an out-of-body feeling. It was that feeling that you never want to end. Each time was different and better. I felt I was more than blessed that he chose me when he came to Kansas. This was the man that I was going to grow old with.

I went to the fridge to grab some bottles of water. I was not going to pay five dollars for a bottle at the beach. Anthony was big on us drinking water, so we always had cases of bottled water at the house. In the fridge was a container of fresh fruit with a note attached to it with my name on it. When I read the note, it said, "Baby, I want you to enjoy your time at the ocean. Don't rush home. I will be OK. Going to the gym or maybe a run. Take this fruit with you and suck the juices out of it while you think about me." This man was crazy. I thought he knew what was on my mind this morning.

I loved his notes. His notes reminded me of a lot of things I never got as a child. My mother never left me a note, and I never got this kind of attention. I anticipated getting a note from him every day. He knew what it took to make me feel special. I loved Anthony more than he will ever know.

I got into the car and headed south to my favorite spot on the ocean. On the way I had turned up the music and rolled the windows down to feel the breeze hit my face. It was a thirty-minute drive, and this morning, I couldn't get there fast enough. There was not too much traffic on the highway. I was surprised. Sundays were family days at the beaches. San Diego beaches were the best beaches I had ever seen. There was always a music festival of some sort going on, and we are always in attendance.

The beach was beautiful and full of people as the morning dew was dissipating. I went to my favorite spot in the corner next to the big palm tree. I get plenty of shade under the tree, and I was always there just in time before the daiquiri man got there. Jose made the best drinks, and while I sat on the beach, it helped me to relax, but it reminded me so much of being in Jamaica. The sun was glistening and starting to beam off of the sand. Every person on the beach had on sunglasses. Today was more special for me, so I had on my Prada sunglasses today. I had on my white Jordan linen short set and black Nike sandals. I had my towel, my favorite towel that I had had ever since I was sixteen. I felt lucky and safe with this towel. It was a University of Kansas towel. After I sat there for a while staring into the water, I lay back and started to stare into the sky. As I stared into the sky, I started having flashbacks, when I was awakened by Jose. He was asking me if I was ready for my next drink.

I had a lot on my mind, and being near the ocean always gave me the peace I needed to figure things out. The one thing that I really needed to think about was a call I received from my old church about a reunion that was being planned back in my hometown of Topeka, Kansas. The message left on my cell was from Pastor Jones. He asked me to call him to get more information. I had not talked to him in over ten years, so it was surprising to hear from him. I was sure he got my number from my mother.

As I sat there, I was thinking about what Anthony's feelings would be about going back home. I was having mixed feelings, but I would like to see Diane, Yolanda, Jermaine, Laquisha and Darryl. I was just not sure how Anthony was going to feel since Jermaine was always trying to provoke a fight with him. My mom wanted me to come home, and I would like to, but if we did go back, we would have to stay in a hotel. We were grown now, and we did grown men things now. I could definitely catch everyone up on the status of my CPA firm and brag on Anthony becoming a consultant. I thought, "I have to convince Anthony to go back to Topeka."

When I got to the parking lot, I found a place to park close to the restaurant that I loved so much. Their hot dogs were to die for. I had only packed some beer and water. I knew that I would be getting some food from my spot. The beach was already getting packed. Lots of joggers and people with dogs running along the beach. I spread out my blanket and got settled. I had my iPad and Bluetooth headphones, but right now I wanted to listen to the waves. If you never listened to the ocean, you were missing out on a very powerful voice that would talk to you and give you advice if you sought it.

When I was comfortable, I texted Anthony to let him know I was OK. The first thing I wanted to do was to call the church and see what the call/message was all about. If it was something I wanted to attend. But first, I wanted to pray and meditate and get my mind right.

"Excuse me, sir, do you have the time?" A White lady was standing in front of me when I opened my eyes. "Yes, it is 1:00 p.m." Wow, I must have fallen asleep. But since I was on Pacific Standard Time, and it was two hours behind Kansas, this would be a good time to call the church. I was sure the pastor was in his office since they were busy with Sunday School and pre-church things. I wondered if the church had grown since I was last there. It was a small community church when I attended as a child.

I picked up my phone and dialed the number. The phone rang about four times; then I heard, "Good morning, this is Mrs. Smith, how can I help you?" Mrs. Smith has been the church secretary for thirty years. She was one of the oldest members of the church. I told her who I was and asked for the pastor. She didn't remember me but asked me to hold on while she put him on the phone.

After holding about three minutes, I heard that voice. That strong voice of Bishop Jones. "Praise the Lord, Kevin; man, it has been years. How are you, son?" I told him I was good and it was good to hear his voice. He then told me he wanted me to come to a church reunion for all of the former members. It was going to be a celebration of his fifty years as the pastor, and it was going to also bring all the old members and folk in the community together. He gave me the date and asked if I would attend. I told him I would get back with him by the end of the week. I had to check my work schedule. He thanked me and told me that it would be so good to see me. Then he said he had talked to all of my childhood friends, and they all were coming. "Kevin, it is going to be a great homecoming, son. I am praying that you can attend." I told him I would do my best and try to attend. I appreciated his call and asked him to pray for me.

Speaking to the pastor brought back a lot of memories. I was thinking of when the pastor tried to convince my mother to have me sing in the choir. When the pastor got on the phone, all he could say to me was how great the reunion would be and that I needed to be there. He would not let me get a word in, and I started to get frustrated. I got to the point that I just listened and would not say anything unless I was asked. This reminded me of being a child. I was being chastised and told what to do. I was respectful and rolling my eyes and thinking, "Damn, will he just shut the hell up."

When I hung up, I sat there for a minute and thought about going back home. I was in a mixed state of feelings. And what would Anthony say? I would not go back without him. I would talk to him when I got home, but right now, I wanted to enjoy my time on the beach and leave everything that was not about peace of mind.

On my drive back home, I wondered if some of my friends would be attending. Some I wanted to see and a few I didn't want to ever see again. So, I called my mother to see if she knew anything about the reunion and who was going to attend. She picked up. "Hey, Mom, how are you?" "Hey, baby, I am fine, just getting ready to head to church. How are you, son? What brings on this call so early in the morning? You OK?" "I spoke to the bishop, and he invited me to the reunion. Can you tell me anything about it and who is coming home?" She told me that she had attended a planning meeting about a month ago and was on the committee. She said it was going to be a fun day and almost like a family reunion. She said, "All of your old friends are coming." I wanted to ask her about certain friends but decided not to. She still lived on the same street and knew everything about everybody. She could tell you about everyone's business having never been in their house. My mother was nosy.

The way I felt about some of my old classmates might stop me from attending. I told her I was going to talk to Anthony about it and would let her know if we would be attending. Before we got off the phone, she said, "I love you, baby, and hope you will come home. It has been too long."

When I pulled into the driveway, Anthony was in the yard watering the grass. He had his shirt off just like he had when I first met him in school; he still was a beautiful, muscular, dark man who made my heart skip. I sat there for a minute just looking at him. He saw me and waved. I got out, and he asked me how my day was, and did I feel better? I laughed at him and said, "Yes, baby. I feel much better, but seeing you is what really makes me happy." We both laughed and went into the house.

Our house is a beautiful but typical floral yellow. We had a five-bedroom house that had a nice-size foyer with art on both sides of the room. On the wall to the left was a black-and-white picture of Malcolm X while he was speaking, and to the right was a large picture of Langston Hughes with his usual big bright smile. It led to the staircase that looked like a scene from *Gone with the Wind*. To the left of the staircase was the kitchen that was huge like I liked because I loved to cook. All of the appliances were stainless, including the stove that sat in the island right in the middle of the floor. To the right of the stairs were our offices; my office was larger than Anthony's because I had more work to do than he did. We also had a pool that we loved to get in on those hot nights. We both loved to swim in the nude. Most of the homes in our community had pools, which was typical here in San Diego. The weather and hot nights made it a must-have. And we used our pool all the time. I never had a pool or access to one growing up, neither did Anthony, so we always used our pool. I asked Anthony to meet me at the pool and to make sure he was not wearing any clothes.

I was at the pool when Anthony arrived. He was late. I said, "About time—what took you so long?" He said, "What is this all about?" with a smile on his face. I said, "It is about you and me, and I also want to discuss something with you." I jumped in the pool, and he jumped behind me. We were playing and splashing water on each other, and he was trying to grab me and pull me close. I got away twice, but he caught me the third time. As he pulled me close, we started kissing, and I could feel his manhood on my stomach feeling like a pole. It was jumping and turning me on. He turned me around and held me, and I could feel it between my buns. I was melting like ice in this pool of love. He was whispering in my ear, making me conform to his demands. We started to make love like whales. I know it sounded like a mating call because I was in heat. I needed me a dose of Anthony this evening to keep my mind right. He always knew how to make me happy and please me the way I needed pleasing. This time he was pounding me like a mallet on a steak. I had a little tension that was now gone and me smiling. I said, "I love you, baby. Thank you for being my husband and making me so happy. I am going to take a shower and fix us some dinner. I want to talk to you about a phone call I got."

We showered and met in the kitchen. Anthony was talking to me as I prepared our dinner. I decided to make tofu spaghetti with just sauce and vegan pasta. I also made side salads and garlic bread. While I put everything together, Anthony opened a bottle of Merlot and poured each of us a glass. After putting the pasta on, I turned to Anthony and told him of the call I received from the bishop in Topeka. He asked me, "What did he have to say?" I told him that he invited us to come back home for a reunion. I also told him what he said as to why it was important that we be there, and we would get the details when we got there. I also mentioned to him that I spoke with my mother who told me that all of our classmates were coming. I mentioned that I was eager and would like to go but wanted to know how he felt about going back to Topeka. He said he wouldn't mind because we had not seen our parents in a while. I was happy to hear him say that, but I also wanted to remind him that Jermaine was going to be there as well. He said, "I am cool with that, but if that nigga gets out of hand, I am going to beat his ass old-school style. I just want you to know that. I don't like him, but I am going to remain cordial." "Thank you, baby, but you scare me when you talk like that. Tell me, what do you want me to do? Do I have limits? What can I do, and what can I not do?" "Hell, yeah, you got limits, I don't want him in your face, and I better not catch any sneaky shit. You are more than welcome to have fun with our friends but be respectful." "I will, but baby, I don't want Mario in your face. I know he wants you, and I cannot stand his ass. He is a cheap ho." "You are my man. I promise to stay cordial as well." "Baby, I will tell you this—I do wonder sometimes if you would have chosen him if the circumstances were different. You do not have to worry about Mario, baby. It is nothing like that, and

I promise when the time is right, I will tell you why that will never happen." "OK, baby, lets toast to the reunion. I love you." I fixed dinner, and we ate, listened to some music and went to bed. I slept like a baby.

Chapter 3

Anthony

L et me tell you about the love of my life. I did not meet Anthony until his mother moved them to Topeka.

Anthony Dixon was a young man from inner city of Chicago. He was a troubled young man who had been protected by his mother and father since he was a young adolescent. Anthony was the son of Jake and Constance Dixon. He had no brothers or sisters and had always gotten his way. Anthony grew up on the South Side of Chicago. His mother, Constance, was a social worker while his father Jake worked odd jobs. His parents were having problems. Jake always cheated and played women on the side. He was a player from way back who was refusing to be a role model for his son because this was all he knew. Constance had caught him cheating several times but stayed with him because she felt he needed to be there to teach Anthony how to be a man, and she wanted to keep her family together. She was trying to cope with Jake's cheating as much as she could but did not know how much longer she could hang in there. She was thinking about a change of scenery to where the pace was slower and was more family oriented. She was requesting a transfer to Kansas and told her husband that this was the last chance for him. She was refusing to deal with his cheating ways and women anymore. She gave him an ultimatum and a date for him to decide his fate.

Anthony was born on February 15, 1970, in Chicago,

Illinois. He was the only child but was not getting the attention he needed. Growing up on the South Side of Chicago, he found himself hanging out with gang members from the Disciples. His mother always preached the importance of being a great student, graduating from high school and going to college. His dad really did not have an influence on him other than how to take advantage of women. It was obvious to Anthony that his dad did not love his mother, and he thought it best that he took to the world on his own. He loved the attention he got from the guys in the gang but perpetrated that he was nonchalant and was a bad boy. He liked the attention because one of the guys in the gang and him had a close relationship on the low. Yes, it was true Anthony liked boys, but he liked guys with street swag. He had a thing for dark skin and bubble butts. He and his boy Mario were sexing three to four times a week in abandoned buildings on 115th street when they skipped school. His mom never knew, and his dad did not care.

The neighborhood Anthony grew up in was called Beverly. He lived on W. 97th Street. The neighborhood was nice where every other house had a basement. All the houses in the neighborhood came in a variety of colors, but the thing about this neighborhood was that most of the kids were always trying to do music of some sort. Anthony was 6'1", 175 pounds, had a thirty-inch waist and was very toned. He had beautiful, big eyes and dark-brown skin with a bald head. The shape of his head was so beautiful that everyone, men and women, wanted to touch his head as well as be in his presence. His swag was a gift that drew people who wanted to instantly be in his presence. When Anthony started to hang out with Disciple members, he totally changed. He was becoming a boss and a leader for something he really did not believe in, but he soon would do anything to stay in the presence of Mario. He and Mario had a relationship that was special and could not be broken. Anthony started to fall in love. He only dealt with women for show. He would have sex with some of the girls sometimes, but his sex was for Mario. Mario was what made him happy. Anthony did not care about school and was skipping pretty much when he felt like it. If he went to school, he was doing just enough to get by. He was suspended twice his freshman year, four times his sophomore year, one time his junior year and six times his senior year. Anthony was rising in the gang by this time and was robbing and killing people who made him mad. If he was not in control, he would make you see it his way. In 1987, when his mother decided to move to Topeka, Kansas, for a change of scenery and his safety, he was not happy with that. He could not imagine his life without Mario. When they left for Kansas, Anthony was withdrawing and acting out because he wanted to stay. He had developed feelings for Mario and did not think he could ever have this kind of sex ever again. He was acting out so bad, he and his dad came to blows. He thought of himself as being more of a man than his father. He loved his mom but could never find the way to express to her who he was as a young man. He did not want to leave Mario. He even asked his parents if Mario could move with them. He convinced Mario to ask his mom if that would be OK just in case his parents said yes. He was growing up so fast, and his parents were not ready for what was to come. He was willing to do anything to keep the relationship he and Mario had. Mario was dealing with so many things that he really wanted to come, but he did not want to leave his family. He felt like he would be betraying them. The Hispanic culture was really family oriented, and they would sacrifice what was necessary for family. There were a lot of issues between these two young men, but they did not really understand life for what it was.

He could not imagine getting the kind of love he and Mario had anywhere else. When his mother moved to Topeka, she moved into a neighborhood called College Hill. She liked the area and the neighborhood because it was a prosperous neighborhood. At least, she thought it was. All the kids in this neighborhood went to Martin Luther King High School.

When Anthony's mother enrolled him into school, he was walking around and bullying the other kids. He was spewing his street swag all over the place. He was going to class and disrupting the teacher, but he did see a boy he wanted. He really thought that this was a guy he could love. He wanted this kid and was determined that this kid would be his new boyfriend and he would control his every move. He was strategizing as to how he would approach him and make it happen. When he got his attention and they started to hang out, Anthony was seeing him at least four times a week like he and Mario were doing. He was determined they would be together for life. He wanted Kevin as his property. When he saw Kevin, he thought he was cute but not masculine enough to be seen with. He made up in his mind that Kevin was going to be his boyfriend. If he saw Kevin talking to another guy, he would step in and interrupt the conversation or threaten them. He literally beat a kid down in front of everyone and told him, "I do not want to ever see you in his face again. If you talk to him, you need permission from me." He told Kevin that his booty belonged to him and him only. He even threatened him prison style by saying if he caught him talking to another guy, he would fight him. Anthony was not like the other kids; he was more like a man. An adult in a child's world is how you would think of him because he was very experienced when it came to sex and mind manipulation. He put the fear of God in Kevin where he would not dare talk to another guy, and he would soon be cooking dinner for Anthony. Kevin loved the idea of being controlled. He did whatever Anthony told him to that was within reason because he too was falling in love. Kevin loved bad boys, and he only told his best friend his secrets. He told Diane everything.

You see, Anthony originally came to Topeka with a thug mentality with the thoughts of taking over Topeka. His mother moved them here without his father with the intention of him getting his life together and so he would grow up without criminal activities in his life. He still had swag, but he had changed from the original thoughts he had in mind. He took all of that energy and made it work for him. He knew that he could not see me unless he went to school and he graduated. My parents did not know I was sneaking around with him and having sex the way we did, but I think they had an idea. He started out where I was doing his homework, but he started doing his own work and having me check it for him. He started to focus on goals and would ask my opinion about them. He had turned out to be quite the man. I was sure he had impacted my life more than I could imagine. After all, not everyone could look like a Greek god.

I had fallen so in love with him, and I started to lose focus. I had gotten to the point that I got used to him telling me what to do, and I would just do it. I really felt like one of the girls, and I had the best boyfriend. I was so scared to come out, but I told Diane everything. Even when he made me cry when he told me he was going to find another guy to be with. I did not know why I let him do this to me, but he knew how to work me. Turned out he was the guy for me, and I loved him.

Chapter 4

Our Flight

I called my mother and told her that we decided to attend. I asked her if she would inform the bishop that Anthony and I would be in attendance. She was so excited to hear that I was coming home. Anthony also called his mother to inform her that we would be coming. She too was overly excited, and we were going to try and have all families together for a family day. The main reason Anthony agreed to go back to Topeka was that I agreed that we would go to Chicago to visit his family and friends. I had never been to his home or met any of his family other than his mother. I also had only heard about his friends but never met them. He was skeptical for several reasons, but I understood. He told me that he was now ready for me to go with him to see where it all started.

The morning of our flight back to Topeka was kind of crazy. Last night Anthony and I sat up talking about coming back home. He made it clear to me again that the only reason he was going was to support me and to make sure that we had family time with our parents. We were also hoping that nothing crazy was going to happen. We both had a lot of good and bad memories here in Topeka.

We talked about some of the funny times we had growing up, and we were looking forward to seeing the old neighborhood and to seeing how fat and ugly some of our school friends had gotten over the years. There had been class reunions over the past thirty years, but we had never attended them. Our careers kept us busy, and we really had no desire to come back to Topeka.

Coming out of that part of our lives to where we were today was difficult, and it required both of us to grow up and to develop a relationship that was now as strong as ever. It did not start out that way as kids, but we made it. To return to Topeka would bring back a lot of memories to both of us. That was from the time we met in school, our friends, and the beginning of our relationship. Thinking of just how rough around the edges Anthony was when he first came to Topeka and his gangsta ways, I could remember just how much of a bully he was and the way he treated me. He treated me like a high school girl and made it a point to let it be known that I belonged to him. To let it be known, I liked the way he treated me. He made me feel so safe and secure, but my dad would have killed me had he known that. I used to sneak him in the house and cook him dinner. It was amazing to know that this was now my husband.

I packed my luggage yesterday while Anthony was still packing today. We got into a mini argument because I told him, "Please pack your clothes tonight." He just refused to do the right thing. He pulled out all these damn clothes to pack, and he could not decide from those what to pack. I laughed and said, "Come on, Ms. Ross, with all that wardrobe." We were only going to be there for a weekend, not a month, and he had more bags than me. He loved being the best dressed and looking better than anyone else in the room. He told me that he wanted to show everyone that he was still the best dresser today just like from back in the day. I told him that most of our old friends would probably remember him as a thug-ass nigga from Chicago who scared everyone. "Like it really meant something." He laughed and said, "I am still that nigga."

Our flight was scheduled for a 3:00 p.m. Pacific Standard

Time take off. Kansas was 2two hours ahead of us, and the flight was scheduled for around three hours. The airport was a fifty-minute drive in traffic from our home. We were pushing time to get to the airport, park and get checked in through security. Our only saving grace was it was Thursday, and we did not have to worry about a lot of traffic. The airport should not be crowded. San Diego was a navy city, so there were always navy men coming and going. The navy made up most of the flights and the economy for San Diego. We were booked on Southwest. To me, Southwest Airlines was better because of the zones, and you had room for bags, and you did not have to pay for bags unless you had three or more. They were a natural low-price airline. In fact, Southwest was the number one low-price airline in the industry. Anthony hated Southwest because on one of his flights he was stuck in the back due to him arriving late. I didn't tell him we were flying Southwest until we got to the airport. I did not want to hear his mouth because I knew he would bless me out.

We loaded the car, armed the alarm and were on our way. On the way to the airport, Anthony was on his cell talking to one of his clients about a project he was working on. I loved the way this man took care of his business. He was a take-charge kind of guy who did not take any bullshit. He shot straight from the hip. He loved his work and made it his motivation. He loved his company and his work. He would never let his company go lacking. He was telling his client that when he got back, he wanted to host a dinner at our house and wanted them to meet his spouse. We were an out gay couple, but we kept things conservative. We had nothing to hide, and we both maintained that we would not live on the down low or lie about our relationship. We were both successful and expanding our business on a broad scale. The work and our reputation for the work we did in our community were known around the city. We were well respected in our community.

When he hung up, he said, "We are going to host a

semiformal dinner party for about ten people when we get back. Can you help me with that, baby?" I said, "Sure, baby, what would you want me to do or prepare?" "I want you to pick a caterer and the menu. We are going to make this a red-carpet event to remember. This event will put us toward the top of the business chain." He smiled at me, squeezed my hand, and said... "I love you, baby." I said to him, "When we get to Topeka, we are going to have fun and enjoy all of our family and friends. I am excited about going back Topeka because I will finally get to see what it is looking like after all this time. I have been wondering what all my old friends are up to." I was hoping to see them all, including Mario. Anthony and I were discussing what to say to him if he made it. I looked at him sideways and kept my jealousy inside. This was something we said we would never do, but I told him how much I hated Mario. Mario was his first real love or crush he had when they were growing up in Chicago. Mario was his first male experience. I understood that experience and what that meant, but I could see that Mario wanted something more with my husband. Anthony really could not see that Mario was in love with him, but I did not want to rehash that argument. I knew Mario was his first male sexual experience, and Mario was someone who I really did not care for when we were in high school. I was having palpitations thinking about this. I found it interesting that he wanted to see him first... I was wondering, "Is Anthony having feelings for Mario, and I do not know it? Why is he so excited to see him?"

We arrived at the airport, and everything was smooth. No traffic, we found a good spot in long-term parking and the security line was not long. On the way to our gate, I wanted some coffee, so I told Anthony I would meet him at the gate. I stopped at Starbucks and got a tall caramel macchiato, and as I was headed toward the gate, my cell rang. It was mom. "Hey, Momma, wassup?" She asked if we were on our way. I told her that we were at the airport and we should be arriving around

9:00 p.m. "Will you guys be staying with us at the house? No, Mom, Anthony and I decided to stay at a hotel, and we have a reservation." "Why a hotel, baby? We have all this space, and you can save some money staying with us. I am not happy with that, and I am going to tell your father because we really want some time with you." I told her that we would be spending a lot of time at the house, but staying at a hotel would make us more comfortable. She said, "I understand but you need to be coming to the house. You make sure Anthony knows that I am not going to fight with him over you." We both started laughing. I told her that I loved her and that I would call her once we landed. "Love you, son, and I am so happy you and Anthony are coming home to the reunion."

Anthony got on the phone and called his mother, Ms. Constance. She was happy to hear from him but was super excited when she heard he was coming back to Topeka. He was telling her why we were coming back and that we were all going to have some family time. This was the first time I ever heard him stick up for me in a forceful way in telling his mother how much I meant to him and what we would be doing when we got to town. He was telling her all about his business and what he had planned. He asked his mother if she would come over to my parents' house when we got there so we could all sit down, eat and chat. He expressed to her that this was important to him. He also told her that he had something he wanted to discuss with her when he got in.

"Southwest Flight 202 is now boarding" came over the intercom as I approached the gate. Anthony was already in line, so I just joined him. As we approached the plane, I asked him if he was ready. He said, "Hell, yeah, but I really cannot wait to see my momma." I told him that my mom called, and we chatted and talked about where we would be living. He said, "What did you tell her?" I replied that we would be living in a hotel, but we would be spending a lot of time at the house. "By the way, did you tell your mother we were coming?" "Yes, I did and that we are going to set something up. We need to set something up with your mom and my parents at our house. We can do that."

He said, "That is not a problem, baby, but I am wondering who my mother is seeing. I know she must be happy, but I do not want no thug-ass nothing nigga with my momma. She all I got besides you." "She will be fine, just like us." "I cannot wait to see your parents, especially your father. Me and OG got to talk about some thangs." "What you want to talk to my father about?" "Mind your business and stay out of grown-folk business." "You are crazy; do not be talking crazy to my daddy." "We may have to get away and talk, but we are going to talk about some things. A nigga cannot wait to get on this plane, sit down and catch some Zs. Wake me up before we land, baby, OK? This nigga done put me on watch—ain't that about nothing? It's all good, though."

I wondered what he wanted to talk to my father about. We were already married, so I wondered if he was going to tell my father that, or would he ask him for my hand in marriage? We agreed that we would tell everyone when we were back at my parents' house, but knowing Anthony, he must be over the top. I loved him, but I hoped he did nothing that would totally surprise me. We were about to land, so I needed to be waking him up.

Chapter 5

Home Sweet Home

When we left the airport, Anthony and I went straight to the hotel. While riding, Anthony and I were discussing how nice it was to be back in Topeka. We both were wondering how everyone looked, what they were doing and what their lives had come to be. We both were wondering how Diane was doing. Diane was my best friend in the whole world. I could remember the many nights we spent talking about my boy troubles and me crying about Anthony. I could not wait to see her. I called my mother to inform her that we were going to check into the hotel and would come to the house after we got settled. We checked in at the Holiday Inn Express. We stayed at the one on SW Robinson Avenue, which was a good distance from my mother. I wanted to make sure she would not just pop up in us when she felt like it. I knew it had been a while since I had been home and saw my mother, but she was still that woman who did what she wanted to do. When we got to the front desk, there was this young man working the desk who had flawless skin. I was not sure if he was African or American Indian, but his skin was a beautiful dark skin that I could only imagine was silky to the touch. I instantaneously stared at him when Anthony said to me, "What in the hell are you looking at?" I said, "The desk clerk, OMG, I love his beautiful skin." Anthony looked at me in a jealous kind of way, meaning I have to stroke his ego, so he stayed calm.

"Baby, you are the sexiest man, not only in this hotel, that I have ever seen." I was looking at his skin because it was flawless. I made sure he understood that I was only giving him a compliment. I had to make sure he knew he was in control, so I asked for permission to speak to the guy because I wanted to know where he was from and what his origin was. I wanted to know his name and where he was from. He didn't mind, so I did. I politely said to him, "Excuse me, sir, what is your name?" He said, "My name is Akeem." I said, "Akeem, where are you from?" He said, "I moved here from New York, Jamaica, New York. I am Jamaican. I was born in Jamaica on the Ivory Coast. When I was of age, I moved to New York to live with my aunt. After being here for five years, I decided to make my own way in a different place, so I decided to move to a place where the pace was so much slower and I could get myself together. I have you guys checked in. You are in room number 482. Please enjoy your stay. If you need anything, please do not hesitate to call the desk, and we will be happy to assist you with your needs." I said, "Thank you so much," but as I walked away and looked back at him, I could not help but think, "What was his story?" God!!! He was so damn fine and had a good attitude with great customer service.

We went to our room, we unpacked and we thanked God that we had arrived safely on this journey. I looked around the room, thinking just how classy this room was. The king-size bed looked more like a California king, and I had never seen one of those in a hotel. The frame was a beautiful maple with matching accessories (dresser and chester). The closet was made out of maple wood that was accented by Indian art carved into the wood. We were talking and gazing into each other's eyes, and Anthony started to get frisky. He came over to me and grabbed me around my waist and started whispering in my ear. I laughed at what he was saying and said, "You are a nasty boy." He picked me up and threw me on the bed. I loved it when he did that. He then started to kiss me. The kissing got intense, and before you knew it, we were making love. I loved the way he handled me because he knew how to make my body feel so relaxed. After making love, we took a nap. I woke up screaming; before you knew it, it was five o'clock. I was like "Anthony, get up! We are late, and you know our parents are looking for us." We got up, I called my mother and told her we would be there by 6:00 p.m., no later than 6:30 p.m. She said OK and that she could not wait to see me and Anthony. We showered, changed clothes and headed down to the car. As we got into the car and started to drive, Anthony's phone rang; it was Mario. I noticed Anthony's face changed while listening before saying, "Baby, its Mario. Mario is in town for the reunion; he wants to see us." I had this skeptical look on my face along with a fake smile while I said, "Great. Tell him he can meet us at my mother's house." They talked for a few more minutes before Anthony ended the call. There was a moment of silence before I asked, "What's wrong?" Anthony said nothing and then went into this rant of how he could not wait to see Mario. He started to reminisce about the times when they were in high school in Chicago before they moved and their friendship here in College Hill. He then started to talk about the times when they were gangbanging together. I just looked at him and pivoted to tell him that I was going to call my girl Diane and see what she was up to. She picked up the phone, and I said, "Hello, stranger." She started screaming and said, "OMG, is this my husband?" I said, "Yes, it is, I need you to come to my mother's house tonight. We are having a small get-together."

We get to my mother's house, and she greeted us with long hugs and kisses. She went on to say how much she missed me and that twenty-three years was a long time to be away from home. We were sitting down in the dining room, which still looked the same as I remembered. The table was a big, old, oak table with matching chairs. The brown was a beautiful light brown with the matching china cabinet and hutch. While we were talking, Momma was thinking of one thing, feeding us. She fixed both of us this big plate of ribs, potato salad, greens and corn bread. She could not forget the strawberry Kool-Aid. As we were eating, Anthony was going crazy, saying, "Momma, I love this food. It is so good. Kevin does not cook like this at home. I think he is trying to starve me sometimes with all this kale salad, green beans, carrots and tofu. I always ask for the real food. We are going to have to make more trips to see you." She goes, "Thank you, baby. I know you all wanted to eat some real food that was going to stick to you." I told her that I spoke to Diane and I asked her to come by and Mario was coming as well. She said OK and wanted to know if any of my other friends were coming to the reunion. I told her to my knowledge everyone was coming. I told her we were going to the basement to the bar to wait for Diane and Mario to arrive. She said OK and that she was going to her room to watch TV with my father, but she would check on us later. As we were heading to the basement, the doorbell rang; it was Diane. When I answered the door, we started screaming of happiness to see each other after such a long time. We hugged and had to catch up. We went to the basement down to the bar and started to converse about old times and new times. I asked her what she was drinking. She said, "I want a vodka and orange juice." Anthony had a shot of Hennessey, and I had a glass of Merlot. Diane grilled me and was mad because I had not been home in a while and asked why I had not been home. I told her me and my baby were expanding and growing our businesses. I was telling her about the number of employees I had and my thoughts of expansion. As we conversed, I heard the bell ring again, and it was Mario. I greeted him with a hello and asked him how he was doing. He said all was well and wanted to know how I was doing. I told him all was well and to please come in; we were in the basement at the bar. As he got to the bar, he went over to Anthony and gave him this big hug and held it for a long time. I did not like that, but I said nothing.

They did a handshake, and I asked him if he would like a drink. He replies, "I would like a shot of tequila." He and Anthony continued their conversation, and Diane and I continued to talk when she brought up in our conversation some of our high school classmates. She started to tell me about Jermaine and Yolanda. She was telling me that they never got married, had a child, but Jermaine thought he was the king of the world. She was telling me that he and Yolanda changed, but she was no longer taking care of him. He was a sorry-ass man, but something about him had these men and women taking care of him. He still had that body of a god but didn't have a job and always had the latest in fashion and cars. I really did believe he was a prostitute. "What did you see in him?" "As a matter of fact, they are together now. Can I call them over so you can see them and see what they are looking like these days?" "Yes, please call them and tell them to come to my mother's house." Diane called Jermaine's phone, not Yolanda's, and he answered. She proceeded to tell him that Anthony and I were in town and at my mother's house. She then asked if he and Yolanda would like to come over. He said yes and that they would be over in twenty minutes. We were giggling like high school girls when I said in low tones, "Who is he sexing now?" She laughed and said, "I bet you want some more, don't you?" I laughed and said, No, I got my man." In my mind, I was picturing how Jermaine looked and how he acted. I heard the doorbell ring again, and I answered the door. I saw Jermaine, and he took my breath away. He had those muscles and that beautiful, dark skin; I had a hot flash. I was thinking, "Take me right here, Daddy." I spoke to him and Yolanda and invited them in. I told them, "We are all in the basement at the bar." She walked in first, and I was talking to them between the two of them, and he grabbed my butt. He whispered in my ear: "I miss you." I got weak and lost my composure because I liked his touch. I am not supposed to be doing this, but it brought back memories of him being my first. I could not be a part of this drama because I loved Anthony and I would never hurt him. I do not know why I am even thinking of these things, but I remember how Jermaine used to sex me. I wanted it all the time. We got to the basement, and I introduced them to everyone. Anthony had this look on his face. I asked him, "What's wrong?" He said nothing. Then he pulled me aside and said, "I do not like this nigga Jermaine, and you know it. If this nigga looks wrong at you one time, I am kicking his ass. I know he wants you still, but you are mine—you got it!!!!" I said, "Yes, but I am not looking at him." He stared at me, no words. I knew what that meant and tried to keep my distance. Jermaine and Yolanda got a glass of wine and started to ask questions of everyone, especially me and Anthony. They asked, "What are you guys doing in San Diego?" I responded, "I have my CPA firm, and Anthony does construction." Jermaine had the gall to ask Anthony if he would give him a job; my baby looked at him with a frown on his face, and I immediately said, "Jermaine, you need to ask him that in another setting; now is not the time." We were drinking and socializing when I noticed Mario being inappropriate with Anthony. I walked over and pulled Anthony aside. "I do not like him touching you like that." He went "What are you talking about?" I looked. "You know what I am talking about. You are my damn husband. I will throw this bitch out. He does not need to be touching you like that." He laughed and said, "OK, baby, I will make sure he stops." Then I noticed Mario and Jermaine talking and was wondering what in the hell could they be talking about. Diane came up to me and said, "Kevin, you know I need some time of my own because we need to catch up without all of this." I said, "I will try to make this happen." She then went on to tell me that Laquisha and Darryl came back to College Hill and took over. They came back like Barack and Michelle and just started to build our community. "I went to planning, and I see our community is going to be the most influential in all of Kansas in the next five years. There are going to be retail establishments and business throughout College Hill. That nigga Darryl is militant as hell like a young Malcolm X. He seems to always have that intense look on his face. All of the gangbanging and drug dealing is almost nonexistent in our neighborhood. They came back with them Harvard degrees and were real movers and shakers. You know, they are married now and have two kids. I am going to call them and see if they can come over." "OK, call them, but you know I was always scared of Darryl. He just looks mean. I even heard that he did not like me." Thirty minutes later, they were at that door and looking serious. They were both dressed dressy-casual, Darryl in a polo shirt and khakis and loafers, Laquisha a nice satin blouse, capri pants and heels. Sister was fly as hell, and I was feeling Darryl's look as well. I invited them in and told them we were in the basement at the bar. I told them to go ahead as I went to check on momma. I called out to her and then knocked on her door; she said, "Come in, baby." I told her I was checking on her and Daddy to make sure they were OK. I told her that all my old high school peers were there and asked if she wanted to come and see them. She said, "Give me a few minutes. I need to talk to your father about a serious matter." I said, "What's going on, Mom?" She said, "There is something that we just need to discuss, but I promise to be out shortly. I laughed and told her she needed to stop being fast and laughed some more. I went back to the basement and told everyone that my mother was coming down to see everyone. In hindsight, I had no idea that my parents were discussing my being gay. She wanted to make sure that my father was fine with me and my friends coming over. As I got downstairs, Diane came to me and said, "You need to watch Mario and Jermaine." I said, "Why?" She said, "I overheard them plotting to come between you and Anthony." I said, "Really." As we were drinking and socializing, Momma came down and spoke to everyone. She proceeded to tell us that it was good to see all of us together again. She said she

hoped we could all stay because there were big changes coming. She then went back upstairs to her room. As Diane and I
were talking, I noticed Mario giving Anthony these eyes, and I
felt Jermaine giving me daggers. When I looked at him, he
made me melt. I was saying to myself, "Bitch, get it together;
you know your husband will tear this house up with Jermaine."
I was trying to get away from him when he followed me upstairs and started to profess this love for me. I was like "Boy,
please, you are lusting and only want to sex me like we used
to. You know I have a man, and you are trying to break us up,
but I am not doing that. Had you come correct, I might have
snuck off with you because I got to admit you still fine as hell,
and you can get it, but not like this." He grabbed me and started to kiss me, rubbing my body, and I started to melt. I was so
weak. My mother came out, and he stopped. I asked him to go
back to the basement while I talked to my momma. We went
to her room, and I told her that I loved Anthony, but Jermaine
was being messy and trying to break us up. I continued by telling Momma how seeing Jermaine brought up a lot of old feelings. I told her he still made me weak, and I didn't need to see
him. She said, "Shit, a man like that, that has that kind of power is dangerous, but that has got to be the best dick. That is
what makes you weak. You know who you love, but you need
to not let temptation control you." It was now 11:00 p.m., and
I told Momma, "I am going to tell everyone to go home, and
we will see them tomorrow at the reunion." She said, "OK,"
and I went downstairs to the bar. I made an announcement:
"Everyone, I would like to thank you all for coming; my momma is sleepy, and we all are meeting tomorrow at the reunion.
It is good seeing you all, but we will catch up tomorrow." They
were all leaving, and Mario was trying to find a way to stay I
told him he had to go and we would catch up with him tomorrow. I looked at Anthony, and he told him to leave, and he did.
Diane said to me, "You better call me in the morning so we can
talk." I said OK. Anthony and I stayed and cleaned up. We

finished about twelve, and I told Momma that we were leaving to go to the hotel. She said, "OK, baby, and I will see you both bright and early." While we were driving back to the hotel, Anthony and I had a discussion as to what transpired. He asked me what was going on with me and Jermaine. I said, "Nothing, what are you talking about?" He said, "I noticed him looking at you all night, and he was looking at you like you was prey. That is the way niggas do when they want something. That nigga still wants you." I flipped the script: "Yeah, like Mario? That bitch was all in your face; he was on your eyes like glasses. He was begging you to fuck him. I know because he did not want to leave. Am I lying?" He laughed and said, "You need to quit; he never said nothing like that." We got back to the hotel and got to our room. I looked at Anthony like a wounded animal, and he relaxed me. We had rough sex for at least two hours. The sex was long, hard, deep and rough the whole time, with him asking me, "Whose is it?" I said, "Yours, Daddy." He went to sleep, and I was gazing at the ceiling and thinking about Jermaine and what he was doing. I loved Anthony, but this crazy Jermaine thought kept coming through my mind. Did I want Jermaine to have sex with me? After all, he was my first. I didn't think so.

Chapter 6

The Reunion (Getting Ready)

Seven a.m. the phone rang. "Hey, Mom, good morning, I heard. What time is it? I asked. She said, "It is too late for you to be in bed. Get yo ass up and get to the church. I need you to stop at the store and pick up a few things for the picnic. I forgot to pick them up getting the house ready for your visit." "OK, Mom." I thought to myself, "This is going to be like the good old days. Me going to the store to pick up things that my mom forgot to get." "What you need?" I asked.

"I need a watermelon, grapes, honeydew melons—get four of them. Also three watermelons. Make sure they are ripe. You know how much I hate a sour-ass watermelon. Also, get some other fruit of your choice. I am making a fruit salad. You writing this down, son?" "Yes, Mom, I got you. Anything else?" "Yes, get some limes and a case of wine. White wine. You know, for those Christians who like to drink." We both started laughing. "OK. Anything else?" If I can think of anything, I will call you or text you what I need. What time can I expect you and Anthony?" I looked over to my husband, who was still sleeping. "We will be there as soon as we get up and get ourselves together. What is the weather going to be today? I have not looked out the window or turned on the news." "I think it is going to be a beautiful day, son. We had a lot of rain this summer, but today might be clear day. But just in case, we will have a big tent set up in the parking lot."

"Give us about ninety minutes. We will stop at the store near the church. That store is still open, isn't it?" "Yes, baby, they still open and still overcharging Black folk." "OK, well, let me get off this phone and get in the shower. Love you and see you soon." "Love you more, son. Hurry your ass up," she said as she hung up.

My mother could be extra at times, but I loved her, and I was realizing how much I had missed her. She was still trying to control and run my life. As we were getting older, I needed to do better and spend more time with her. I was going to make sure that she came to San Diego for the holidays. The house was big enough for her and my father to have their own side. I knew she would love the weather and the ocean. Like me, she loved the water.

Anthony was sitting up now. "You want some coffee, babe?" "Yes, that would be perfect." "What time is it?" "Time for us to get it together and head out. Mom called and gave me a list of things she needs from the store. You want to get in the shower first or me? Or we can get in together." He looked at me and said, "Hell no, you ain't getting my dick hard like last night. We will probably not make it to the reunion if that happens. You go first." "What you mean?" I asked, smiling at him. Especially when I noticed his dick started growing and getting hard. "Man, get yo ass in the shower," he said. "I will order coffee." "OK, if you are sure." Hell, yes, nigga, I am sure..." "While I am getting in the shower, it is a good time for you to call your mother to check on her and see if she is still coming to the reunion." I laughed and headed to the bathroom. I heard him calling his mother and their conversation. She was happy to hear from him, and they went on about how things were going in San Diego. I even heard him offer her the opportunity to come and visit. I also heard them arguing about her new boo. This boy just did not want any man being with his mother. What was funny was he never met the guy but always spoke of how he hated him. This boy was very protective of his mother, but I would not tell him how to feel about that because she was like sacred ground to him. I was going to ask if she was coming to the reunion.

When I got out of the shower, he was sitting on the toilet. I had told him a hundred times that I did not want to smell him taking a dump when I was in the shower. He paid no attention. This was one of his domineering ways that I just accepted. He told me, "If I cannot take a shit in front of my husband, then there is a problem." I just agreed. I quickly grabbed a towel and exited the bathroom and shut the door behind me. I told him to hurry up and get in the shower so we could get to the church. I didn't want to hear my mother's mouth about us being late.

As I was putting lotion on my body, my cell rang. I looked, and it was an unknown number. Normally, I would not answer. I figured it might be someone here. "Hello, boy, yo ass up yet?" It was Diane. She had gotten my number from my mom. "What you doing, and where you at?" "I am headed to the church. They got me supervising the children's area. I got to get those badass kids some balloons and ice cream. What you doing?" I told her I was getting dressed and Anthony was in the shower and that we had to stop at the store and pick up some things before getting to the church. Diane laughed and said, "I see you still a momma's boy. Your mom has you running errands already?" I told her to shut the hell up and I would see her soon.

Anthony came out the bathroom, and when I saw all that meat hanging in front of me, I felt weak and wanted to feel him inside of me. I wanted some so bad, but I had to gain my composure and just touch on it and feel it grow. After all these years, I was so happy to know that we had not lost attraction for each other. I was constantly yearning for him to make love to me, just like he did when we were teens. There was something about his swagger and ultra-masculinity that turned me on.

The bed linens were all over the bed and the floor. We had some wild sex last night. I did not know if it was the liquor or just both of us being horny from seeing our exes. As we were making love, I hoped he was thinking about me and not Mario. Mario did look sexy as hell last night, and I saw the way they looked at each other. Even after all these years, the chemistry was still there. I was not jealous by no means, but I knew this bitch wanted my husband. He was my husband, but at the same time, I was no fool. I knew if he could fuck Mario, he would. Sorry, Mario, but that was my husband and my dick.

I was already dressed in a pair of jeans and one of my college T-shirts, a pair of sneakers and a ball cap. I had laid out for him a pair of shorts and a linen shirt. He liked for me to dress him. He looked at the outfit on the bed and said, "I like that. Thanks, babe." "Let's go. Diane called, and she is on her way to the church and needs our help to set up."

I called the front desk and told them to bring the car around, that we were in a rush. The hotel was busy because of a national conference in the city, and all the hotels were booked. I knew that there would be a wait to get the car this morning. The valet service did not impress me when we checked in. This cute brother who parked the car at check-in smelled like weed. I prayed that he would park the car and not take it for a joy ride.

On my way to the lobby breakfast bar, my cell rang. It was Diane; again she said she had something important to tell me before I got to the church. It sounded serious, so I said, "What's going on?" She stated to me that she wanted me to know that she had a girlfriend and wanted me to meet her at the reunion. She said her name was Carlisa. She had long, flowing hair, jet-black hair. She was mixed Puerto Rican and Black. She was 5'3", ninety-five pounds, size one, but was all lady in the chest. "She is D cup just like I like them. The thing that sticks out to me is that this is her natural hair and not weave. She has a beautiful personality. I do not want you to be surprised, but I was bisexual when I was chasing you in high school. I could never give up women. I can do without dick but not the pussy. I love her, and we been dating for three years. It is serious, and I want you to meet her. When I look at you and Anthony's relationship, I want the same thing. I am hoping we get married, maybe we can have a double wedding." I locked her number in my cell to make sure I had it because we needed to talk more. I decided that I would tell Anthony what Diane just told me but told him to not mention it to anyone, including Mario. This was for her and her only to reveal. She stated that she wanted to talk to me before I got to the church because she felt I needed to know. I was honored that she felt this way because we had not been in touch all these years, but our bond was never broken. I started to feel bad because I was not being a good friend and staying in touch. I would always have love for Diane. She was the one that helped me come to grips of reality as to who I was. She always tried to date me, but I never would but always confided in her. If I had any secrets, I knew she would keep them in the vault and would never tell anyone. I remembered like it was yesterday when she was constantly trying to date me. She always asked me what was wrong with me, but I never would say. She used to joke with me about always being smart and a part of all the school organizations. I just saw her as a good friend. We would discuss movies, TV shows and sometimes books. When I really felt comfortable was when I had all this love for Anthony when he moved to Topeka. I told her I had something to tell her. She said, "What you got to tell me?" I told her, "You know the new guy Anthony?" She said, "Yes, what about him?" I told her that I wanted him and that we were having sex. She said, "What?" I told her the times, places and things he told me. I also told her that I feared him, and he said to me that I was his and he better not catch me talking to another dude. He told me if he caught a guy talking to me that he would beat me and make me act right. I was not going to lie, but that turned me on so much. I just loved aggressive bad boys for some reason, but no one ever knew it. When I left Topeka, I did not intentionally leave and just forgot about Diane, and I got to let her know that I wanted her in my life. She had helped me through a plenty of rough times when Anthony made me cry. I loved her and considered her to be the sister I never had.

Chapter 7

The Reunion (Heading to the Church)

I pulled out my list of things Mom wanted and started my shopping. As I was looking at the fruit, I heard a voice say, "Kevin. Kevin, is that you?" I did not recognize the voice, but when I turned to see who was calling me, my mouth fell open. It was Jermaine. I was thinking, "OMG, it would not do for Anthony to come in here." Jermaine proceeded to tell me how good of a time he had at my mother's house last night. He was telling me that me and Anthony coming back for the reunion brought all our friends back. At least those who'd moved away, and everyone wanted to see me and Anthony. He said many people had speculated many things about us but had no idea what was going on with us. They did not ask anyone about us; they just clearly speculated negative things about us. He told me that there was a rumor that Anthony gave me AIDS. He still would not tell me the person but said also that Anthony was beating me and made me be his boyfriend. The thing that really got me was when he said he would always love me and that I never gave him a chance. I said, "How can you say that when you were my first but always used me to get whatever you wanted from me?" "If anything, I was your bitch. I would cook for you and even buy you expensive shirts while working my summer job for the city. Do you still have the Versace shoes I brought you? I was totally infatuated with you. Even as you stand before me now, I am weak for you." "Jermaine, you cannot do this; you decided to love that White girl, Yolanda, remember? She could buy you more things than I could, and you could fuck her and people not say a thing. I was just your closet freak. Anthony is waiting for me, and you know the two of you are like oil and water. We are heading over to the re-union; I am sure you are heading there as well. See you there, and please do not start any trouble, sir." "Daaamn, you still sexy!!!"

While my baby was in the store getting the items his mom wanted, I decided to walk across the parking lot to the McDonald's. I remember growing up and hanging in this shopping center with my crew, and the only fast food joint was Mr. Pops, who sold hamburgers and hot dogs with soda. He would also have ice cream in the summertime. It was a popular spot for all the teens. We would meet up and hang out and talk and talk to the girls who would be there. Me and my boys would smoke some weed and talk shit. I would tell them about Chicago and how much I missed living there. I was the man and the big-city kid everyone feared and looked up to. I always dressed like I was in the big city. When it came to dressing, I was always on point. My moms made sure I had all the latest gear.

As I entered the restaurant, it was long lines. Damn, first, I did not eat fast food, and, now, I had to stand in line. I pulled out my cell to check out my Facebook page and to send my mom a text and let her know I was heading to the reunion. I had just talked to her, but I wanted to check and make sure that she was still coming. As I was looking on my Facebook page, I noticed some of my former classmates popping up in my suggested friends list, but I was finally at the counter. "How can I help you?" the young sister with the long braids asked. I looked up at the menu again and said, "I will have the egg white sandwich. No meat and a water. In fact, give me four sandwiches." I thought Kevin would be hungry, and if he wasn't, I would eat them. "Also, give me two of those fruit cups." "Is that all?" she asked. She gave me my total; I put my card chip up in the credit card machine and stepped aside to wait for my order.

I was still on my cell when I heard, "Get the hell out of Dodge, if it isn't fine-ass sexy Anthony from Chicago." I looked up and said out loud, "Damn, it's Cee Cee. The loudmouth sister who I attended high school with." She still looked the same. A plus-size light-skin sister with a ton of jewelry on and about five earrings in each ear. Now she had her nose pierced. She came up to me and hugged me and said, "Nigga, where you been, and what you doing in this tired-ass town?" I laughed and said to her, "You are still as hood as you were back in the day." "Hell, yeah, nigga, a sister going to always keep it real. So, wassup?" I told her about why I was in town and asked if she was coming to the reunion at the church. She said, "I don't do church, baby, but if they going to have some food, I will be there and bring my four kids. A bitch ain't trying to cook." She laughed, and I laughed. Then she asked me, "Where is your lady at? I know your fine ass got bitches all over the country and about ten kids." "Fool, you are crazy," I said. Then I got a text from Kevin. "I am in the car. Let's go."

They called my number for my order, and I said, "Hey Cee, I got to go. We are running late to the church." "Who is we?" she said. I told her, "I will see you and your badass kids later at the church...and you better be there. Bring some friends as well because it is going to be a great day of food, fellowship and catching up with our old gang." "OK, baby, I will be there. I need to go change and get my act together."

I headed back to the car, and Kevin was looking around, and the car was running. I got in and asked if he was hungry. He said, "Yes, thanks, baby." I opened the bag and gave him a sandwich, and we headed toward the church. In the car I told him about running into Cee Cee. He asked if she was still loud and a hood bitch. I laughed so hard I almost spit out my food and said, "Some things don't change. You will see for yourself. I invited her to come out today, and she is bringing all four of her badass kids." "OMG," he said, "this is going to be a remarkably interesting day. I hope we get there on time and don't have no drama." "Something is telling me that we are going to have some trouble. You know things are crazy when you run into a bitch like Cee Cee."

Chapter 8

Arriving at the Church

As we drove down Main Street to the church, we were talking about where we used to hang out and looking for places that were still the same. When we came to a light, we both looked up, and right in front of us was a billboard with the pics of Darryl and his wife, Laquisha. It said, "Welcome to the new community of Living Life." They were smiling and looking like money. "Wow," I said, "they are doing the damn thing. I am so excited to hear about the plans today." Mom and Pastor had told me a little about what they were planning on announcing today, and that was one of the reasons for the reunion.

Anthony said, "Yes, this should be interesting to see what they have in mind. This community needs a shot of energy and life." We pulled into the church parking lot, and there was already a lot of people there. I saw the tent, tables up and lots of balloons. I also noticed that the committee had on purple and gold T-shirts. I parked, and we got out the car and started unloading the food. I looked for Mom, but instead, I saw my father. He was standing at one of the barrel barbeque grills. I was nervous when I saw him because I was always afraid of him. He just looked at me. He stood about 6'4", 240 pounds, was bald-headed with this salt-and-pepper beard. "Hey, Pops," I shouted at him twice. I asked, "Why are you looking at me like that? Did I do something wrong?" The music was turned up, and I knew he was hard of hearing. He turned around and got this big smile on his face and said, "Son, come give your dad a hug, boy." I was looking crazy like, did he hear me? "Hey, Pops, I see mom and the committee have you doing what you do best, cooking the meat." " Yes, Lord, they know how to use my skills; no one at this church can burn like me, and you know that." We laughed, and I asked him where Mom was. "She is inside with the kitchen women." "OK, I will get back with you later, Dad. I got all this stuff for her." "Where is Anthony, son?" he asked. "I think he went to the restroom." "I will tell him where to find you."

I entered the church and could smell all the food coming from the basement kitchen. I stood in the lobby for a minute to take it all in. I grew up in this church, and it still was the same. Nothing had changed in the sanctuary. I closed my eyes for a minute and thanked God for allowing me to come back. It felt so good.

As I headed down the stairs, I ran into Mrs. Smith coming up the stairs. "Hello, Mrs. Smith," I said. She looked up at me and said, "Praise the Lord." She did not recognize me until I said, "I am Kevin, Diane's son." She said, "Boy, you are all grown up. Well, look at God." She hugged me and said, "It is good to see you, son. Your mom is down in the kitchen." "Thank you," I said, and I headed into the kitchen. "Hey, Mom," I said when I saw her sitting at the table peeling potatoes. "Hey, baby, why you late, and where is Anthony?" "He is coming, and here is some of the things. I am going back to the car." "OK, hurry up, baby. I got some things I need you and Anthony to do for me." "OK." As I headed back to the car, I looked over and saw Anthony standing talking to my dad. That was a good thing. I hollered at him to come help me get the rest of the food out the car. He shook Pops's hand and headed to the car. "How was that?" I asked. "It was good. We talked about sports and Cali."

He grabbed a few bags, and I took what was left, and we headed back into the church. Mom told me she needed us to set up some more tables in the tent and put out some chairs. I asked her where the bishop was, and she said he would be out in a minute. He was meeting with the trustee board about the plans that were going to be announced today about the new development.

We brought changing clothes to the church because I knew my mother would have us working like crazy. We went to the restroom to change into our reunion clothes. After getting dressed, me and Anthony went out to see if there were any last-minute things we could do before people started arriving. While doing some touchups, I looked, and I saw Diane and this pretty Puerto Rican girl. They were looking like they were right out of a magazine, Diane looking nice with her hair freshly done and her friend looking like a Puerto Rican goddess with long, flowing, jet-black hair. They were cute with their purple shirts on. The women wore purple shirts, and the men wore gold shirts. She and I began to talk, and I had to ask, "Who is this girl? I do not know her—is she new in College Hill? Who are her people because I do not remember any Puerto Ricans when we were in school." She said therefore, "I have been telling you we need to talk. This is my baby, boo thang, lover or soon-to-be wife." I said, "What? Bitch, you got a pretty one. I do not see any other girl in College Hill coming close to her. What is her name?" "Carlisa, Carlisa Rodriguez, and, Kev, I love her to death. She makes me so happy, and we are trying to do some things. We are trying to stay in the good graces of Darryl and Laquisha. You know they are running this bitch now. Let me introduce you to my baby. Lisa, I want to introduce you to my high school friends; this is Kevin." "Nice to meet you, gorgeous. Girl, you are so damn pretty. How do you put up with Diane's ass, lol. This is Anthony, my other half." "Nice to meet you, Lisa; daaamn, you pretty as hell." "Let me tell you all something that I have not told anyone, including my parents. Anthony and I are married." "What? You never told me and didn't even invite me to the wedding? Wassup with that? I am going to let yo ass get away with that this time, but the next time I am going to have to beat yo ass for breaking the friend code. I am so happy for you all, though. Anthony, how do you put up with Kevin and his perfections? Remember how he was in school? He used to get on everyone's nerves with his know-it-all ass. He is my nigga, though. We are going to come and visit you all soon." I looked up, and I saw goddamn Jermaine and Yolanda. This nigga was just determined to make me cheat. OMG, that gold shirt looked so good on him. It was gripping him like a glove, and he was wearing these khaki pants that were just show-ing everyone his business. You had no choice but to look as it was just lying to the left and almost to his knee. My mouth was watering, and I was speechless and just looking. Anthony was going to get me. Yolanda was cute with her purple shirt and gold capris on. What was captivating was the purple-and-gold Prada shoe boots that were three-quarters the way up her legs. I greeted them and this damn Jermaine was in my ear again. He asked me if I wanted him to hook me up. He said, "I saw you looking, and I know you want me up in that booty again. Let Daddy know when you get out of jail; you need to run from that nigga. I am still waiting." I could not believe that every time he did that, no one saw it. "Jesus take the wheel; I love my husband, but I really do want to get another taste." I hated him, but he was so sexy, and he knew me. I was such a whore right then. Acting like a Stepford wife—what was go-ing on with my mind? Anthony was every bit as sexy and had a body that just didn't quit, but there was something about Jermaine that hypnotized me. I was trying so hard to avoid him. He was being mean-spirited, but Yolanda was so nice. "Kevin." I turned, and it was Anthony calling me. I looked at him like a deer in headlights; I was so scared that he saw what happened and he was going to chastise me. I was about to cry, when he said, "The ladies need some help in the kitchen." I said OK. I went to the kitchen and looked at my mother when she said, "Baby, do we need to talk?" I said, "Yes ma'am." We went into the medical room of the church, and she asked me what was going on. I said, "Momma, Jermaine came up to me and said some things to me that got to me. He still wants me; I am happily married, but I want to have sex with him again." She asked me why. I said, "I really do not know, but he knows a part of me that no one does. I need to scratch this itch, but I am so afraid that Anthony will not understand if he finds out." "Baby, leave that boy alone; he is no good for you and is trying to break up your home." "Yes ma'am. I will just stay away. I really don't see him as that kind of person, though." I said, "Momma, give me a few minutes to gather myself, and I will be there to help you all in the kitchen." As she walked out and closed the door, I started to cry. I wanted to have sex with Jermaine so bad, but I was so afraid of Anthony finding out. Jermaine came in the door, and I was so turned on. This nigga was such an opportunist. He knew how weak I was, and he came right in and started kissing me. I could do nothing but let him have his way. He started to whisper in my ear, and it was turning me on. He said, "I am going to make love to you like a real man does it." He started to undo my pants and was kissing on my neck, and all I could do was look and be paralyzed. When he got my pants down, he flipped me over and inserted his dick inside me. I started panting and relaxing as all of him was inside me. I was loving this for two reasons: I was not supposed to do this, and we were sneaking to do this. I knew who I loved, but this was my first. It reminded me of the time when we were in high school. I was so scared, but I liked this. I thought about the first time and said we needed to stop. We were in the office for thirty minutes, and, boy, was I rejuvenated. Jermaine kissed me and said, "Do not worry. I won't tell yo nigga. This is my present to you because I know you all are married. We cool, but I would love to be boyfriend number two. I want to be the maintenance man; let me know wassup." He left me there, and I was still gathering my breath, but I knew I had to get back out there. I ran to the kitchen, and Momma asked me where I had been. What had I been doing? I told her I was praying. As I was helping them with the food, Anthony came in and said, "Kevin, Darryl and Laquisha just arrived." I said, "Cool, I am coming out to greet them." When I saw them, they were just so extra; they were not wearing the T-shirts like everyone else. Laquisha was wearing a beautiful Vera Wang purple dress and the prettiest shoes. Darryl was wearing a custom Versace old gold suit that was clinging to his muscular body. As we were chatting and exchanging pleasantries, Darryl said to me, "Kevin, what we got planned includes you. I want you to really listen to what is going to be announced." I was looking puzzled but wondering, "Is this the same Darryl?" I said OK. I was thinking like "What is going on?" I looked up, and I saw the pastor and the first lady. They were coming in like celebrities, shaking hands and kissing babies. The pastor went over and started talking to my mother and father. My dad was talking about how good his ribs were as he was calling everyone over to see just how good they looked. As he was doing that, I saw, of all people, Cee Cee. As usual, she was on CP time, and she had her four badass kids. She was just as Anthony described her to be, loud and obnoxious. I had to say hello. Then just like always here came queen Mario. Bitch thought he was going to take my husband. I greeted him with a lot of shade, but he went to talk to Anthony.

The pastor then went to the stage and started the reunion. He went, "Can I get your attention please? I would like to thank all of you for coming out for this reunion. This reunion is for our community and the people who make up the community. There was a proposal brought to me by some people in our community proposing we take the lead in the state by building our community and making sure it is the leader of the state of Kansas. It is factual that because our community is 98 percent Black there is no way we can make our community the leader of this state. Well, the plan that was proposed is very progressive and has more than just potential. Two of our own have come back to us because they believe that our community has more than potential to grow and make a change that will be life-changing for all here in College Hill. Two of our own left home, went to a prestigious university and have come home to give back. I am talking about Sister Laquisha and Brother Darryl. These two young people have come home from Harvard University to bring upward mobility to our community and to help put us on the map. Without further ado, I introduce Laquisha and Darryl to tell all of us about the plans for College Hill." "First of all, we would like to thank you all for coming to this reunion. It has meant so much to me and my husband, Darryl, to always build our community. Since we first started to date when we were in high school, this has always been a vision for us. We have envisioned our community being a leader in the world as well as in the state of Kansas. We all know nothing is given and nothing works if there is not a good team in place. When we graduated from high school and went to Harvard, we decided that we would come back to College Hill and grow it. We contacted the pastor and talked to him about all the things we have seen that could be done here in College Hill. We envisioned that our community needed shops, malls, cafes and condo high-rises. We learned that our community sits on prime property, and we could not let outside forces come here and dictate what is coming in and going out of our community. We came up with a plan in four phases and came to the pastor and asked him for his assistance in getting this done. I will let my husband finish with the plan that has the start and conclusion dates." "Thank you, my brothers and sisters, for coming out today. We are here to tell all of you of this great community as to what is coming and what the end game looks like for College Hill. I want to start by giving a special shout to Kevin James and Anthony Dixon for making the trip here from San Diego. These two brothers are going to play a major part in the development of College

Hill. As my wife previously stated, building College Hill will be completed in four phases. Phase one consists of retail shops, office spaces and condominiums. The retail shops and office spaces are going to be right at MLK and the interstate. The retail spaces will be uniquely built in multiple buildings that will go as high as fifteen floors. We have actually coordinated with all major retailers like Saks, Neiman's, Macy's and Prada to put stores here in our community. We will have all the coffee houses, and the office spaces will be in buildings at least twenty floors tall. The spaces will be reasonably priced for all to come and put their offices in our community. This will bring an enormous amount of money to our community to stimulate it, and wages will be more than what our state demands for hourly work. We are looking at salaries starting out at $85K and hourly wages at eighteen dollars. As you can see, this is way above what you are used to people making in the entire state of Kansas. We negotiated that in order for these shops to come into our neighborhood, they must employ a lot of labor from this community, and we will be checking the stats to see if they are holding up to the contract. If not, we have a clause to move them out of our community. We are looking at unemployment in this community alone to be at least 1 percent. That is unheard of but true because we are going to have job training and vendors who will be doing certification courses for those who do not want to go to college but get the equivalence. There will also be vendors who will do job training for the many companies up to tech training to make sure you get a job. The next thing that makes this special is Kevin is a CPA from College Hill and has a thriving practice in San Diego. We would love it if he could help us by doing the stats and track the progress of all four phases and be a part of the accounting functions in a compliance manner. We are also hoping to have him come home and open a location here in College Hill. Let us know, Brother Kevin, if you are OK with helping us. Brother Anthony has a large construction company in San Diego, and we would like for him to bid on the contracts for construction and build these lavish buildings that we have in the plans. We would like to hear from both of you brothers soon so we can push forward with phase one. I thank you all for coming out and supporting us and the community. I am turning it over to the pastor for final words." "Thank you, Brother Darryl. Ain't God good? Thank God for the blessing of this young lady and young man to have come from our community and to be so smart. It is amazing that kids as young as you can love their home and want to do something about problems that they did not cause. We all should more than give them a hand, but we should be their biggest supporters. If you all want to socialize and eat, the food is ready, and I thank you all for showing up and showing out as we are going to show this entire country what a Black community can do when we come together." I was like "I am so glad he is done," and I ran instantaneously to Diane. I said, "Girl, this place has been so full of drama. I love what Darryl and Laquisha have put together, and I am going to tell you first: me and my boo will take them up on the offer." I loved home, but we needed to go somewhere quiet and talk. We walked to the pastor's office and sat down to talk. I was talking in a low tone, and I told her that me and Jermaine had sex in the nurse's room. She screamed and said, You are lying!! I said, "No, I am so weak, and I feel so guilty for doing this. I wanted it, and he just kept messing with me. When he came up in here with his dick hanging to his knee, I wanted some. Don't get it twisted: Anthony puts it down, and got more dick, but Jermaine was my first, and I wanted to get a taste so bad. Please do not tell anybody because this could destroy my marriage. I will make the announcement back at my mother's house when we all leave here. What should I do?" "Stop being a slut, lololol!! Nah, but just play it cool; what did Jermaine say?" "He said he would not tell, but that was my present, and he knew that we were married. I did not know how he knew that. I did not confirm this, but I was shocked. He also said that he wants to be boyfriend number two." I didn't know, I didn't like fire, but Jermaine was fire, and I knew he would burn me. "Let's talk more when we get to Momma's house. Thank you, everyone, for coming and enjoying. I am inviting you all back to my mother's house for drinks and celebrating."

Chapter 9

Reunion at My Mother's House

As we arrived at Momma's house, I was feeling guilty and happy at the same time. I was guilty because I knew I was dead wrong, but I was happy to know I still got it and Jermaine still wanted this. I had no idea why I wanted his attention, but sometimes I felt like I needed his validation. Maybe it was the way he treated me that made me feel less than a man when we were growing up. As we got to the house, I told my mother and father that I wanted them to be out front when everyone got to the house because I had an announcement for everyone. I went to Anthony and told him that I was going to make the announcement that we were married. He looked at me and said, "Are you ready to do that?" I told him yes, because it was time for us to move on. We were grown and did not have to hide from anyone. He said OK. People were arriving, the pastor and first lady, Darryl and Laquisha, Diane and Carlisa, Mario and Jermaine and Yolanda. We looked and saw a car coming down the street that no one recognized; it was Anthony's mother, Constance. He ran like a little child to meet her and ask her why she did not show up to the reunion at the church. She apologized and told him that she just did not come because she knew how he felt about her now fiancé. She went on to say that she wanted to make sure she spent some time with him before he went back to San Diego. He invited her in and introduced her to everyone.

I gave her a hug and told her that I was so happy to see her, and: "I am so glad you came. I cannot wait for you to come visit us." I introduced her to my parents, and they started to have a deep conversation. When they all had arrived, I had glasses of champagne waiting for everyone. When everyone got in, I said, "Could everyone please get a glass of champagne?" Anthony standing by my side, I said, "I would like to propose a toast to me and my husband. Yes, Anthony and I are married. We have been married for twenty-three years. When we left College Hill, we left because we were in love and wanted to be married. I hope you all are comfortable and happy for us." There were cheers, but my father had this look on his face. I did not know how to read it, so I went to him and asked him if we could go in my old bedroom and talk. When we got there, he told me, "Son, I love you, and I know I cannot live your life. I do not like this thing of you being married to a man. I am just not comfortable with that. I know this is a happening thing, but I will learn to adapt. Please do not ever surprise me like that again. Grown or not, I will still beat yo ass. Do you hear me?" "Yes, sir," I said. "I love you and your husband, but I do not know what I am supposed to feel now." "Daddy, just be you and love me; that means more to me than you can ever imagine." I gave my dad the biggest hug and said, "Thank you so much for being my dad." I told him, "I promise I will tell you all the news first before I tell anybody." "That's wassup, son. I can deal with that." We went back out to the rest of the party and celebrated and drank. There was no drama, and everyone was happy. My mom and Ms. Constance (Anthony's mom) came to us and told us how much they loved us and congratulated us with plenty of love. They told us how special we were and that they would be there for us if we needed anything. I constantly looked at Anthony and was wondering if he was feeling like I had done something wrong. I knew it was called a conscience, but this was running me crazy. I then did that thing that people do on TV: I was in a daze thinking about the church and just thinking I was such a SLUT!! I was desperately trying to get Diane's attention, but she was too busy talking to Jermaine and Yolanda. I was more than amazed at how he was acting; I really thought that he was going to blackmail me. Therefore, they say people tell on themselves and other people do not have to say a thing. I just knew I needed to talk to my girl Diane. I knew that she would help me to rationalize this and to make an informed decision. I really enjoyed myself with Jermaine, but I was constantly thinking about how he made love to me. I even thought about him and the guy at the hotel, Akeem, and me in a threesome. I have always wanted to do that, but I felt like if Anthony knew or even thought that I was having these thoughts, he might leave me. I loved him, but I really wanted to just get my freak on. OMG, was I an undercover HO? I should not be thinking like this. What I need to be doing was finding a way to tell Anthony what happened and get the rest of this shit out of my mind. I could not wait to get home and relax and get my mind right. I was creating drama, and I hated it. I heard Diane calling me, and I could not wait to talk to her outside. She asked me what was going on with me, and I told her that I had to tell Anthony what I did. I was explaining to her that it was weighing heavy on my heart, and I was feeling so guilty. I told her I was so happy for us to get reacquainted and that I did not think this was good for me to come back here. I was explaining how being so conservative all my life and thinking of wild sexual pleasures didn't match. I was explaining how this place did that to me. We laughed, and she said, "I hope you are not being a ho." She said, "I don't see you like that, but if you are trying to make up for lost time, this is not the time. You are too classy for that, but I know slip-ups can happen. If there is nothing else to it, I say, let it go. If you love Anthony like you say you do, then you will not anything to jeopardize his love for you and your marriage. In other words, thank about that before you go running off at the mouth. That boy may beat yo ass to a pulp if you tell him something like that. You got this, and me and Carlisa are coming out to see you guys in a few months." "Girl!! I love you and thank you for being a friend to me. I am so ready to go home."

Chapter 10

Going Back to San Diego

The phone rang at 6:00 a.m. I picked it up, and it was the wakeup call I requested when we returned to the hotel last night. Even though our flight was not scheduled to leave until 5:00 p.m., I still like to get up and not have to rush. I had requested a late checkout of 3:00 p.m. so we could have lunch and not be rushed out of the hotel at the normal noon checkout time. I wanted to check my emails since I had not been online since we left home. I had a couple of clients I was waiting to hear from. As my company was growing, I also needed to look at hiring some new blood. I had posted on LinkedIn a job description, and I wanted to see if I received any interest. Anthony was in the bathroom. I heard the shower running, so I could take this time to check. So, I logged on.

"This water is so damn hot," Anthony thought to himself as he stepped into the shower. I was still feeling bad about what happened at the church, and I didn't sleep well.

After I showered, I sat on the toilet for a long time, thinking and mentally beating myself up. What made me give in to Jermaine and at the church of all places? I really fucked up. Why didn't I fight him, and why did I let him take over my mind, body and soul? What was wrong with me? I had never cheated on Anthony. I had been approached by many men in San Diego who wanted to go out for a drink or who asked if I was single. I had heard, "You are sexy as hell," compliments from some extremely attractive men. But I never thought about cheating on my husband. I would even tell him when a man would try and get my number. He would laugh and say, "Baby, you are fine, and I don't blame them. But you belong to me. I own that ass." We had the type of relationship where we could talk about anything. That was the key to the success of our marriage. Open communication and nothing to hide.

As I was sitting on the toilet with the shower running, I had my head in my hands, and my mind wondered back to the day we got married and said our vows to each other. It was a long journey to get to that place where we wanted to get legally married and spend the rest of our lives together. I remember the day he asked me to marry him.

It was senior year in high school when we had a couple of stupid arguments about me liking Jermaine more than him. I finally convince him that he was wrong before he apologized. We were like the typical high school boyfriend/girlfriend relationship where I was mostly doing all his homework to make sure he had good grades. The thing that made that so special was that most people did not know that Anthony had made a complete change and was very smart. He did all his homework. I only checked it before he turned it in. He would come over to the house, and I would fix him dinner, and we would always stay in the house and watch movies. When it was time for me to go to college, I was not going to leave him. While I attended the University of Kansas, Anthony went to the junior college. We stayed in between Topeka because the University of Kansas was in Lawrence, and his school was about twenty minutes from my school. We learned to live together and really become a loving couple. I saw him as my protector. He would never let anything happen to me or let anyone look crazy at me like they wanted to harm me. I loved him for that. I felt so special. There was one time some guys came from Wichita and were hanging around the store where we shopped; one of the guys was not only casing the store but looking for victims. Anthony let me intentionally go out the store without him, and the guy surely tried to rob me. My knight in shining armor came out of nowhere and kicked his ass and his two friends' asses. I was screaming and hollering for help and crying because I thought they was going to hurt my baby. I tried to help, but Anthony told me to get back and he got this. OMG, I thought he was going to jail because one of the guys looked like his head was cracked open bad. One of the guys could not walk, and one of them had a shoulder separation. The police came and took them to jail, but we had to go to the police station and give statements. We were released and went home, but I had to ask Anthony where he learned to fight like that. He looked at me and winked and said, "Yo NIGGA got you; you just need to listen to what I tell you to do. I just looked, but I did call my mother to tell her what happened. She asked if we were OK. I told her yeah, but I also told her that Anthony reminded me of a gladiator. I had never seen anything like that up close and personal. He got his two-year degree and got a small-time construction job while I pursued my last two years of my undergraduate degree. Right before it was time for me to graduate, Anthony proposed to me. It was shocking, unbelievable, but just what I wanted. When he graduated, his mother was in attendance, as was my mother and father. We had a small celebration, but his mother was not all the way sold on our relationship. She always gave me the side eye. My thought was "Bitch, he is my man!" I gave it to her with a smile. She knew I was shading her, but there was nothing she could do. He point-blank told her she needed to get on board or just leave us alone. She was trying to and got a little better. When it was close to my graduation before he proposed, he said, "Baby, I got to talk to you." I was trying to put my last project before everything, but he said, "Nah, nigga, sit yo ass down and listen." I said, "OK, what?" He went through the spill: "You know I love you, and I do not want anyone else. I want you to know that the best thing that could have ever happened to me was for my mother to move me here to Kansas. I was hating that shit at first, but when I met you, I knew you would be mine. That is why I am asking you, will you marry me?" I said, "What?" "Will you marry me?" I said, "Yes!! Of course I will marry you." He pulled out a gorgeous band that had diamonds around the whole band. I cried, and he just consoled me. He said we should go to the courthouse tomorrow and get married. I was not thinking but started to think, and I asked, "What about my parents and your mother?" He said, "This is about us, and we will tell them when the time is right." I agreed and said to him, therefore, "I love you so much." He then said. 'We are doing that traditional shit; we are writing our vows." I said, "Anthony, in one day? Can we come up with vows in one day?" He said, "Hell yeah, I am putting those writing skills you helped me with in school to write mine, and you are going to sit down and do the same." "I know you are not going to let me out, do you?" We sat down and wrote our vows, rehearsed them and drank until we were totally inebriated. The love we made was the best. It was so good I could not get enough. I wanted more and more, and he kept giving it to me. Each time was better than the previous time. When we woke up the next morning, we were talking about what our life would be like. We showered, got dressed and went to the courthouse. While sitting there, we got the license, and then it was our time to get married. I was thinking, "OMG, what if Momma found out I was eloping? She would probably kill me. Daddy probably would think we are doing too much, but he would just say, 'Whatever you want to do.'" They called us in; the judge introduced himself and asked us if we were ready. We said yes and started to proceed. When he got to the vow part, he said, "I understand that you have written your vows?" We said yes, and he said to Anthony, "You may read your vows first." He started by saying, "Kevin, to me you are an angel God sent to me to save my life and put me on the right track. When we first met, I was a diamond in the rough that was found by you. You found me, nurtured me and polished me to be the man I am today. You have shown me love and taught me how to love. Without you, I do not know if I would still be alive. I do know that I love you and will always love you. It matters not when or where, I will always be with you. I love you." While he was saying this, I was just crying and could not believe that my baby was a man. He was a grown man who motivated me to do what I had to do. I knew that once we finished the ceremony, I was going to love this man forever and ever. After the ceremony, we went home and celebrated, and I could not stop looking at my ring. I felt so elite now because I was married and I got a husband. We started planning our future and decided that I would get my master's degree in accounting and take the CPA exam, and we would move to San Diego. All of this came to be. This was like a fairy tale. This was hard to believe, but it was really happening. Therefore, I could not believe that I was such a fool. How could I have had an affair with Jermaine? I loved my husband. I could not tell him this because it would devastate him. He might possibly leave me. I could not be alone because I need him if I was going to live. I had to tell him. I needed to have a crying spell when I told him so he could not leave me, pass out and hit my head so he could not leave me or just run out in front of a car. He was looking at me like he knew something was wrong.

"Baby, you OK? Damn, you been in there for an hour. I need to get in there. I got to piss. Don't have me come and do my number two," and he laughed and said, "I thought I was the only one in this relationship who didn't mind taking a shit in front of my husband. Get out of here fool," he said.

"OK, give me a minute. Be right out." I grabbed the towel and opened the door. He was standing in front of me naked with a hard dick. I looked at it, and he said, "So, you want some more before we check out?" I kissed him and said, "I always want that dick. Because it belongs to me. But we need to pack and get checked out. We still must return the car, and it is a holiday weekend." He looked at me and said, "OK, baby, but as soon as we get home, I am going to bust that ass."

As I got dressed, I tried to shake the thoughts from my mind about the sex with Jermaine. My dick was getting aroused with the thought of how he felt, and when he whispered in my ear how much he missed me and even after all these years, he still loved the way I tasted and felt.

"Hey, baby, let's go," said Anthony. When we got to the lobby, Anthony headed to the complementary coffee bar, and I headed to the front desk to check us out and request the car. I had promised Diane that we would call her and let her know we were checked out. She thought maybe she and her boo could meet us for brunch. I did not think we had time, but Anthony did want to tell her bye and to reconfirm she was coming to visit us during the holidays. So, as the clerk was checking me out, I looked for Anthony to get him to meet the valet driver. He was on his cell, sitting in one of the oversize stuffed chairs in the lobby. I could tell he was in a deep conversation with somebody, so I did not want to bother him.

I tipped the valet ten dollars and waited on Anthony to get in. Whoever he was talking to had him really into the conversation. When he got in the car, he was still talking and had a profoundly serious look on his face. I pulled out and tried not to listen in on the conversation. He told the person that he would meet with them on Tuesday at 10:00 a.m. at his office. Then he said, "Bring all the paperwork, and we can go over it. I am headed back to San Diego today. I will touch bases with you when I get home." Then he hung up. I asked him if everything was OK, and he said, "Yes, just business shit. I am ready to get home."

As we drove to the airport, we did not talk much. We were both looking out of the window, and then Anthony started to do some work on his tablet. I was asking him what he was doing; he replied, "I am setting up a big meeting when we get home." He said to me that he was going to possibly need me to host a dinner party. He gave me no details and said, "I will let you know more when we get home. I have a potential big client who wants me to do some work for him. As usual, you know I am going to have you do the numbers and help me on setting the amount of the contract." He said out the blue, "Whatever you got going on in your mind, you need to drop it. I need you to be focused and sharp because if I can get this contract, it puts my business up there with the big boys. We need to be Batman and Robin to make this happen. I also want to know why you are looking so distant and lost. Did something happen? Did you get some bad news? Do we need to talk about something?" I was speechless but lied and said no. "I am good; I just miss my parents and home is all. I apologize for seeming so out of sorts. We are going to get this contract because I am going to check the contract of the last contractor and compare the jobs and put you to the top. When will you tell me more about the client?" "I will tell you when we get home. You should be ready to do your thing because we are going to get this contract."

Chapter 11

Meanwhile, Back in College Hill

It had been a week since the reunion, and the community was still excited about the news that was shared about the big project that would bring jobs and bring back new hope for the entire city. Over the past ten years, the community had some bad times. From the fall of the real estate market to the closing of the biggest employer in the city that laid off a lot of people who lived in this community. Then the rise of crime did not overlook us. We had our share of gun violence. Drugs had made their way into the lives of many of our people, and we saw a presence of young Black men who were causing a lot of our older people to be nervous and scared.

I had many conversations with members of the church about how they wanted to move away. They were tired of hearing about break-ins and someone getting shot for no reason. Like most cities in the country, we were not an exception to the change in the country.

When Obama was elected president, we all celebrated and thanked God for this blessing. We hoped that having a Black president would make life easier on us Black folk. We had campaigned, and we voted for him. He even came to the city, and we had over one hundred of our members attend the rally downtown at the arena.

When Obama gave that speech that night, it was like watching Martin Luther King Jr speak. The way he captured the spirits in the room and gave us his hope for this country made me reflect to the civil rights movement that my family was involved in. It felt good to see all the young people, Black, White and Hispanic, all in accord that he was what this country needed.

I had always wanted to make sure that the young members of my church understood the history of the church and the roles of the elders of this church played in paving the way for them to have the freedom they have.

I needed to call Anthony and Kevin and see if I could schedule a conference call with them and the planning committee to follow up on what the next steps were as it pertained to their involvement with the church. I had decided to ask Anthony to represent the church as our contact working with all the construction companies who would be hired to work on the new development. We wanted to make sure that qualified minority businesses were given contracts to work. I had several members who owned small businesses who could benefit from this new money.

I also wanted to show the members that I supported our LGBTQ members and friends. It took me a while to get past my own personal issues, but I needed to be more open to everyone. I wanted to be an example for all the other pastors who still preached hatred about homosexuality. I would not. Having Anthony and Kevin involved as a married gay couple from College Hill would be a big step for the church. This I knew, but I was willing to stand up and support my decisions.

Anthony and Kevin were success stories from this community, and they were role models on how you could overcome society with small minds and grow to live your best life. That was what God wanted from all his people. To live in truth.

These young men truly were great men that were humble and loved by all, but what made it special was that they were Black men. I got them on the phone; Kevin answered and said, "I am putting you on speaker." He called Anthony into the room, and they greeted me with so much happiness. I once again thanked them for agreeing to help us do this and said that it was wonderful that they would help the community. I started by saying, "Gentlemen, I have Darryl and Laquisha here, and we are on speaker." Laquisha spoke, "Good morning, Kevin, and good morning, Anthony." Darryl followed with "Good morning, guys." I started with "The reason I called you guys is because we are ready to start moving forward with our plans. Our first plans are to get the plans set for KEVANT Construction Inc. and the role they play in this first phase. The deconstruction of the old buildings downtown and the additions to city hall and the parking decks. We have received the plans from the engineer, and we are setting/planning to break ground in six months. We are going to need you and your crew to be in place and ready to go. The funds are going to start coming in sometime next month. This leads me to you, Kevin; we are going to need you and your people, if you are bringing any or hiring in place, to make sure all the funds are accounted for and appropriated properly. Will this work for you guys, and will you be able to make it in time?" Laquisha jumped in and stated to Kevin: "I know you are the man to make the finance work because I can remember how good you were in math in high school. I am so happy that you two have decided to come back and be a part of this growth. Darryl and I have really worked on this and want to do what is best for this community. It has given us so much, and I know we can make the difference that those before us could not. We have big plans when this is done." Darryl, being his strong self, jumped in and said, "I want you guys to come in and really take the bull by the horns. We are looking to be the leading Black city in the country. We being the second generation of our parents will make this city grow up on new-age technology and be the leader of the free world." "We trust in you guys, but I will be pushing to make sure this happens. With all of this being said, it was really great that you guys came back for this reunion. This brought back so many memories for me. I was thinking when all of you were kids and coming to the church, and I had to get on all of you at some point in time, and now to see you all are young professionals making a difference in the place we all call home. I am so happy, and forgive me for displaying the tears of joy, but I am so proud of all of you. For me, a man of my age is so proud to be a part of this and seeing the kids I had a part in their lives grow up like you all did. When can we expect you guys, and when will our next call take place?" Kevin stated that he could make things happen in about a month. He stated that he had a person who could run his firm, but he had to get things set up. He also had to get things set for KEVANT Construction Inc. so Anthony could make arrangement for the heavy equipment he would be using. Darryl yelled out, "Our next meeting will be four weeks from now, 10:00 a.m." Everyone agreed, and I said, "Thank you, guys, for taking the call, and we are looking forward to building our neighborhood. You guys, have a good day. Thanks, Bishop, and we will talk soon."

We now knew that we had a meeting over the phone on January 24 at 10:00 a.m. with Darryl, Laquisha and the bishop. That meeting, we would have to display that we were ready with the equipment and how we would be getting it there. We also knew that the groundbreaking was in July. We were going to have to make plans for both our companies in our absence. We started doing this instantaneously because Anthony said he could have the plans done in one month. We were going to have to live in College Hill temporarily, or we could purchase a condo or house as our second home. We needed to discuss this.

Chapter 12
Always Something

My meeting was scheduled for 9:00 a.m. at the W Hotel on the pier in downtown San Diego. I was meeting with my team to discuss the dinner that Kevin and I were planning to have at our home. We were inviting over one hundred people who were clients, associates and local leaders. I wanted to tighten up my business relationships, and what better way than a fabulous evening at our home.

In San Diego, it was all about showing success. These White folk loved to be impressed and dress up. Even the Black business community was very upscale and did business with their kind. Kevin and I were part of the community of movers and shakers. We had not ever done anything this big at the house, but the house was beautiful and big. I wanted to spare no expense to roll out the red carpet. Kevin had given me his blessings, and we had set a budget of $100,000 for the event. It was an investment in our future. And would come back threefold or more.

My team consisted of my VP of operations, VP of finance, VP of administration and four college interns who worked for us in the summer. Even though I didn't have a four-year degree, Kevin was highly educated, and he supported making sure that young people had opportunities to learn. So, when we added the internship program to our company, we received applications from local colleges and chose four of the best. Two White and two Black students.

I had left the house early to get to the hotel to make sure that everything was ready. I ordered a breakfast and had reserved the VIP conference room. Kevin was already gone. He always went to the gym at 6:00 a.m. to work out. I told him all that damn food we ate at the church and his moms's made both of us gain extra weight.

When I got in my car, my cell rang. It was a Chicago number but no name. I turned on my Bluetooth and hit answer. "Hello."

"Is this Anthony?" the female caller asked. "Yes, who is this, may I ask?" "Hello, sir, my name is Monica, and I got your number from your mother." "My mom," I thought. "What is this about?" I had not talked to my mom in a few weeks. "Is everything OK?" Monica said, "Yes. No problems. She wanted me to call you to ask if I could email you a document that needs your signature." "What kind of document, and why hasn't she called me?" "I don't know, sir, but if you could give me your email address, I will email it to you today."

I gave her my email, and she said to look for an email from her within the hour.

This concerned me. My mom had said nothing about this or anything. Strange. But, again, my mom can do some shit that surprises me sometimes.

As I pulled into the W valet parking, I decided to text Kevin and tell him about the call. He didn't respond. Must be working out or in the shower.

I walked up to the front desk and told the lady I had an appointment, and she made a call to the catering manager who came down to escort me to the forty-ninth floor, where the conference room was.

On the elevator, I didn't say anything to her. My mind was still on the call from Monica. When we got to the floor, I had received a text from Kevin. "'Sup, baby?" it said. I didn't respond because the catering manager wanted to go over the meal and meeting details.

I was thinking, "What the hell am I here for if she called him about the menu?" I asked the young lady if she could give me a minute because I needed to make a call. She said no problem. I called Kevin and asked him what in the hell was going on. "What did you guys discuss because I am here to make sure this thing is like I want it to be. and I do not want to double talk." He told me that they did not discuss any details because I was coming for the meeting. I said, "Thank you for that, and I am still thinking about this call I got from this lady named Monica. She says my mom asked her to call me and to email me a document for me to sign. I gave her my email address, but I am going to do this meeting and hit you back."

The young lady was genuinely nice and professional. She started, "My name is Anita, and I am the banquet specialist to make your event unforgettable. Let me first let you browse over our products, and when you are ready, we will do your consultation and then your selections, is that OK?" I said sure. As I start to browse, I noticed the proteins, and they were grade A, all of the veggies were organic and freshly prepared, the breads looked really good too. I got to thinking, "Am I going to run over the budget?" I told the young lady that I was ready, and we discussed what I wanted. I told her that I wanted the filet mignon and Cornish hen for meats; I asked about the veggies because I wanted to make sure I make it look extravagant. I asked about the cauliflower, broccoli, carrots and then a vegetable medley. I then asked about the asparagus and Brussels sprouts, and she told me they were all fresh and organic, but: "I recommend you do the asparagus and cauliflower. There will not be a lot, but they are filling and make people feel like they are not eating a lot." I decided to take her up on that. I picked two breads, yeast rolls and the regular dinner rolls, and Caesar salad. I told her that I needed this to serve two hundred people, and I needed them to be at my house by 4:00 p.m. to start setting up. She explained that this was not a problem and that she would add this up for me.

She told me the total was $8,000 with no servers and $10,000 with servers. I laughed and said I needed the servers.

After taking care of that, I called Kevin and told him the damage and that I was feeling strange. I could not get Monica out of my mind, and I wanted to impress my potential client but also the people of College Hill. I told him that I would see him at home, and if he could please have me a drink ready, I would really appreciate it.

Chapter 13

Never Say Never

During the festivities, Anthony made sure he greeted every single guest. And he also made sure that I was introduced to the guests as needed. The ones he wanted me to know, I met. Others, who were not in his circle—it was not that important for me to meet. But we both were the perfect hosts all night. The surprise was Jermaine was there, and I was still not understanding his story as to how he was out in San Diego. I started having hot flashes and crying spells. I figured that he was going to pay me back.

When the mayor arrived, who was an out gay White man married to a Black man, that was the highlight of the evening for me personally. Even though there were lots of gay and lesbian guests attending, having the mayor and his husband attend was the cake topper. The mayor was only thirty-nine years old, and his handsome, sexy, dark-skinned former navy officer husband was my age. They were well liked and had done a lot for the LGBTQ community. When he won, it was because of the gay community. The city of San Diego had never had that kind of voter turnout ever. Anthony and I attended all the post-election parties as special guests of the mayor. My company and Anthony's company both had written big checks to the candidate. We also had attended all the fund-raising events that many of the LGBTQ leaders led.

Even though the Black gay community was not that big

in San Diego, the ones who were there were not on the DL or still stuck in a closet. Our circle of gay men was out and very outspoken successful members of the community.

At the dinner, many of our gay friends attended and told us on their way out that we were the new gay power couple.

When I finally said good night to the chef and his team, I had taken off my shoes. They cleaned up everything. His team made sure that the kitchen and all the serving areas were spotless. The tent was still up, but the bars and the band were gone. All the candles were out, and the string of lights was also unplugged. The house was not quiet. Just an hour ago, there were close to two hundred people there. It was a success.

Where was my husband? I called his name and didn't get an answer. So, I headed outside, and there he was. Sitting on a chaise lounge talking to Jermaine. They were drinking wine and talking. What are they talking about? I wondered All night, I had avoided Jermaine. Every time I got close to him, I turned and went the other way. I didn't want to have any interaction with him.

Anthony called me over to tell me of the conversation he and Jermaine were having. He said that Jermaine was really a cool guy and that he was changing his thoughts of him. He was telling me the story of Jermaine's flight being canceled. They then turned the conversation to economics, and Anthony was trying to explain supply and demand. While drinking that damn Hennessey, his speech was really slurred. He then proceeded to ask me to explain economics to Jermaine because I knew that shit so well. "Go ahead, baby, explain that shit." I proceeded to explain it to him, and he was looking directly into my eyes. I was so uncomfortable and felt like Anthony was going to catch him doing this. While still talking economics, I proceeded to put my head on Anthony's shoulder and was playing with his chest. When I started to explain inflation and deflation and its relation to pricing, Jermaine decided to ask a question. He wanted to know how this affected employment.

He said there was no way this could affect employment because it sounded like people were just spending money. I stated to him that it played a major part because it determined salaries and employment rate and interest rates. I explained, It's all about supply and demand. If you have more supply, the demand is less, and there is an unnecessary surplus that causes prices to drop and companies in certain industries off workers. If you have less supply, then demand is high, meaning prices rise and employment is sturdy, and no one is losing jobs. The economy is good." I knew Jermaine was doing this to be messy, but it was cool. This bitch was making me sweat, dance for dollars, and was controlling me like a puppet because he knew I was scared. I showed him to the downstairs bedroom that I had prepared for him. I was so glad he went to bed. I asked if he needed a wake up to make sure he got to his flight on time.

He said no but wanted me to know that he was cool and he was not here to cause me harm. He laughed at me and said, "I would never hurt you because you will always be special to me. Yolanda is not here because she has some things to do with her mother." He then asked me if he could have some booty. I looked at him and said, "Are you crazy?" He said, "I know you want some more because you were throwing that ass back like crazy in the church. You can get it anytime you want it. I told you I have no problem being your number two. You really don't want nothing to do with me? You can tell me the truth." "I cannot answer that question right now. Boy, you are going to get me in trouble." He grabbed my hand and put it on his snake. It was so big, and I wanted it, but I knew this was not the place or time. I told him, "Just be cool, and if we do anything, it will be when we get back in College Hill." He said, "OK, but you better not be playing with me." I said, "I promise, and I am not playing with me." I said, "I got another question for you, though; why do you want me?" He said, "Because you have always had your head on straight and was about your business, but you got ass that is just like pussy. It is to die for; that is why your boy loves you so much. I guarantee it. We good but the next time, I am going to knock it out the box!! Guaranteed. I want you to dream about me tonight."

Chapter 14

The Morning After

It was 6:00 a.m. the next day, and Jermaine was awake. I asked him if he wanted some breakfast and coffee. He said yes and that his flight was leaving at 9:00 a.m. I put together a quick continental breakfast, fruit, bagels, croissants and cheese, and let him brew his own coffee via the Keurig. There was enough for at least six people. I did not eat a lot, but Anthony and Jermaine gobbled down an enormous amount of food. He ate and left for the airport about 7:30 a.m. He had plenty of time to catch his flight, which was good. I told him that if he ran across any problems to give me a call. He said one thing to me that really caught me off guard: he asked me to ask Anthony if he would hire him. I told him that I would ask him, but he would be calling him to give him the answer.

I spoke with Anthony and passed on the message from Jermaine; he looked at me and said, "Are you serious?" I said, "Yes, he asked me to ask you, but I told him I would, but you would be calling him with the decision." Anthony went on to say that he had had a change of heart about Jermaine. He asked me if I would have any reservation if he did give him a job. My mind was running faster than the best computer processor. I said, "No, as long as you are comfortable, I am comfortable." My self-talk was saying, "If you say no, he is going to ask why. But if you say yes and put the ball in his court, he will be fine," and that was what happened. I asked him if he was ready to move on from the high school issues between the two, and he said yes. He said that he was thinking that after a while he could use Jermaine as a foreman back in Topeka because of him knowing all the people back in College Hill and the city as a whole and that he had connections that could help his company really grow. I said that was great and I supported this 100%. I did not hear from Jermaine, so I was sure he made it to his destination. I was so glad that there was no drama. I loved Anthony with all my heart. I was wondering, though: would he really hire him? What was that conversation about that they were having at the gathering last night? What would he do if he found out Jermaine sexed me during the reunion? I had to be honest with myself: I was nervous about this whole situation because I saw them running into it again. I was thinking about just last night, when I was showing Jermaine the room we prepared for him to stay in, he was trying to do me in my house. Hell, I thought that would be cool, but I could not be so easy. I was just thinking about how sexy he was and that I loved the way he treated me and dominated me. I just wanted to have all the cake and ice cream in the world, if it was my secret. I could never get caught because that would be the end of my marriage, but living dangerously was not that bad.

I called Diane because I had to tell her what just happened. When I told her that Jermaine was just here at our house and he stayed overnight, she was baffled. She asked me if I was trying to get killed. I told her no, but I did not know what to think. I told her that Jermaine told me that he was out this way because he wanted to get away. He told me that Yolanda had something to do with her mother, and she could not come. It was his story, but it sounded fishy. Anyway, I told her about him telling me that he would be my number two if I wanted him to be.

She said to me, "Kevin, you need to be careful and stop trying to live on the edge, because you know that is not you.

If you are not careful, something bad is going to happen, and that is not a good thing. Stop letting temptation push you to do things you know you don't do. I am telling you this as your friend who loves you and cares for you. Don't fuck up what I got going on and start acting crazy. Love you, and I will talk to you later."

Chapter 15

Guilty

Things were now back to normal. We were on our regular routine. The event was such a success that we made the society column of the local newspaper, and even the gay newspaper did a story about us. The headline read, "Power couple host major event." San Diego was a very White city; few Blacks had status. That was in both the LGBTQ community and politics. To be given this kind of press was major. Anthony was busy with his new client who signed a multimillion-dollar deal for his company to build the new arts center. Jermaine had not started working with him at the San Diego office but was officially hired as the new development director for the Topeka office, where we would be working on the new development and also serving on the board of the church's development board for all new development that would impact the community. The bishop wanted Anthony to be a part of all future projects. We had not looked at a place in Topeka to live yet. I asked Diane to look for a condo or maybe an apartment for us to call home there. She told me that there was a new high-rise opening in downtown that I would love. The apartments were big and started at $4,000 and up. I told her to check it out and get back with me. My mother wanted me to buy a house near her. Property was at a good price, and we could get a big house for a great price. I didn't want to buy a big old house; we would only be in Topeka a few months out of the year, or Anthony would be in and out, but we needed to find something by the first of the year.

Anthony told me that he was happy about everything, and he wanted us to take a short vacation soon somewhere to relax. He knew I loved the ocean, so he said maybe we should go to Hawaii. I told him wherever he chose would be fine with me. He also told me that he wanted Jermaine to come out to San Diego for a meeting with his team and meet some of the associates he would be working with. I asked him, "Why don't you just do a webinar conference call instead of flying him out here? That would save you a lot of money because that is a unnecessary expense. Video conferences seem to work for a lot of companies." I was trying to keep Jermaine away from us, especially me. I still was feeling something about him. I didn't want to admit it, but I had been dreaming about Jermaine and us making love. And if truth be told, I would make love to him again. Yes, I said it. I really would.

Anthony told me he needed him in the city and had his assistant book him a ticket, and he would be staying with us for about a week. "A week, damn, a week," I thought to myself. "OK, baby, that is fine with me. Business is business, and you know I stay out of yours. I am going to work on finding us a place in Topeka and getting the guest bedroom downstairs ready for Jermaine."

I got on the phone and called Diane because I needed some Topeka tea and to see where she stood in looking for us a place. I dialed her, and she did not pick up until the fifth ring. She said hello; I said, "Hello, heffa, what took you so long to answer the phone?" She said, "Hey, baby, how are you?" "I am fine. Tell me what you have found so far." "I have not found a good place, but I do think that since you guys are looking for a temporary place that I will look more for some apartments. I got to say, Boo, I think you all should just purchase another house here and be dual residents of both California and Kansas." "Why do you think that would be best?" "Because you guys will be here for these projects in all four phases, and it is going to be a lot of work. All you guys need to do is just be here, especially you, with all of that financial stuff you will be doing. I am most looking forward to you all coming back because I am missing our friendship. That reminds me, I need to tell you about my girl. Kev, I love her to death, and I want to tell you first I am in love. I am getting to the point that I cannot be without her. I dream, sleep and think of her 24/7. We are living together, and we are not having any drama. Our communication is good, and there are just no complaints. I do worry though, is that possible? Is that a problem in itself? I am not trying to sabotage my relationship, but I know I love her. I figure that I will just go with the flow because I know we both feel the same. What do you think, Kevin? I need to know your opinion because you are always giving advice, lol. I do not think that no one can have a relationship and not have arguments. That is a part of growing together and shows compromise. If there is no compromise, then you cannot have a relationship. No relationship is perfect, and if you guys communicate the way you say you do, then you should talk about it. I need you here because I want what you and Anthony have. I want to get married. When I look at you guys, I see happiness, but I also see a lot of love." "You know I miss our friendship as well, and I think you may be right; we should just buy a house in Topeka and call it a day. I am going to talk to Anthony about it and let you know. In the meantime, please start looking for houses for us in College Hill." "I need to tell you something too, I was doing some research of College Hill. I found that College Hill looks like it is really in Wichita instead of Topeka. I am not sure because we are so close, but I have always thought of Topeka. Hell, they stole the land from the Indians and now this." "Hell, I am still looking, but also, I did something that I am so scared to talk about." "What did you do?" "Why I had to do something?" "I know you!!" "Let me go outside. I had an affair with Jermaine." "What?" "I had an affair with Jermaine. When we were at the church having the reunion, he did me in the nurse's room. Diane, I feel so guilty for this. I love my husband. I tried and tried to resist Jermaine, but he kept coming at me and just wore me down. Girl, I am so sorry for this and cannot find the time to tell Anthony what happened. He feels so comfortable with Jermaine that he has hired him. He is making him one of the big people in his company in Topeka. I am asking you to please not judge me and to cut me some slack. I was so wrong, and now it looks like I have caused my own destruction. I got to tell you this though, girl, he still got it. That nigga had me calling his name and sweating like crazy. I am so glad you did not notice my eyes looking like a deer in headlights. Girl, I felt like such a ho but a good ho. I felt good because I know I still got it. He assured me that he would not tell, but he is also controlling me from afar. I am starting to believe him, but I don't want to get too comfortable with him either. On a better note, I want you to know I will talk to Anthony about us buying a house in Topeka. You are right, girl; we should just buy a new house in College Hill, and we pick up on our friendship. I will convince him, so please find us a house and let me know. By the way, what is the latest with Darryl and Laquisha?" "Well, I heard that they are both about to enter politics after phase one of College Hill. I do not know this to be true, but I heard Darryl is targeting the governor's house, and Laquisha the US Senate. I can say they are a real power couple, and I am sure they will be successful after you all get College Hill where it should be." "When you see them, please tell them I said hello and to please give me a call. Also let them know I am anxious to talk to them as well as see them." "I will, and I love you, baby." "Love you too." We hung up, and I headed back into the house.

As I got back into the house, Anthony greeted me and told me how much he loved me and that he could not live without me. My self-talk was "OMG, he must know." I just kept acting normal, and I said to him, "Baby, I told Diane that she should look for us a house instead of an apartment. I think it will be a good idea for us to have dual residency in California and Kansas. We can live at home from time to time and come to California when it is cold in Kansas. I think it will benefit both our businesses and put us in a better tax bracket." "If you think it is best, baby, we can do that. I agree with you, and I say, let's do it. Are we going to look or have your girl peep the scene for us?" I was sure our parents were going to be shocked to hear this. Besides, the thought just ran through my mind that we would be in Topeka for an extensive period establishing business for both of us. "Nigga, we are doing what the White folk do. Let's get this paper. You with me? Yes, you better be. Make me get that ass if you had said no, lol." "Boy, stop, you are going to make people think you are beating me. I am going to prepare the room for Jermaine and work on our business taxes and get ready to incorporate our businesses in Kansas." "That's my baby. I know you got my back, and I can trust you." "Baby, I am so blessed to have you in my life. I would not be in this position if it were not for you. When I get through with this room, I need you to be in the room resting and waiting for me. I got a surprise for you." "OK, what is it?" "Nigga, just go to the room and wait for your baby." "Don't be too long, or I am coming to fuck you in that room." "You are so crazy; I promise not to be long." I got to the room, and my baby was glistening in the freak red light. He was looking like a Greek god with that beautiful dark skin. OMG, I was such a weak bitch; he just looked at me, and I cracked. He started to pull me onto the bed, and I fought to get away because I was going to give him a strip tease, lap dance and then this good ass. I started to strip, looking like a ho on the pole and working it well. I was throwing this ass just like my baby liked it. I then started to take off clothing, but I did it like a real ho. I knew he liked that when he was horny, so he could beat the brakes off my love tunnel. I loved it when he was rough with me. This was when I knew I belonged to him. After being totally naked, I turned around and dropped it like it was hot on his lap. I was grinding like a real bitch in heat. My baby was so hard, you could take that wood and hammer anything in the wall. I was so excited but realized that I was in trouble because he was going to punish me. When feeling that wood, he was going to make me submit to him like no other time. He picked me up and dumped me on the bed and started to kiss me real hard. He then started to kiss my neck and nibble on my nipples as though if they were grapes. I was moaning like a dog in heat because I was hotter than a furnace in New York City on a real cold night. He then tasted parts of my body that had me shaking. I heard him whisper, "This is the cleanest plate I have ever seen." He then inserted his probe into my receiver and started pumping the well slowly. He then took off and had me out of my mind. I was speaking in tongues. I was panting and moaning and screaming like a banshee. He was doing me like he never did me before. He hit all my spots, and it seemed like he hit the spots five times each. I was calling his name and screaming, "Daddy, I love you." He was driving me crazy. I did not want this to stop. He was always good, but tonight he was the heavyweight champion of the world. My baby was the champion, and I could put him against anyone's husband. I got the best husband, and he loved me. There was no woman or man getting it like this. I was already doing what he asked me to do, but now if he asked me to run in front of a car, I would do it. He more than rocked my world—he controlled me like a video game, and I loved it. I was his husband and his bitch. I knew I satisfied my man. He made me so hot, I needed another round. He made me beg, which I did, and he really punished me. That was the best pain I ever experienced. I had orgasm after orgasm, and it was everywhere. I had no more energy, and I was breathing very hard. My baby worked me and made sure I did my duties to serve him. He then leaned over and told me to make sure that the alarm was set and the house was secure. I responded like a little soldier and did what

I was told. I could not wait to call Diane tomorrow and tell her what happened. I always loved the day after because the feeling of soreness was a turn-on. Especially if he caught me off guard and just got a quickie. I fell asleep instantaneously.

I woke up with a big smile on my face. I looked over at my baby and said good morning; he responded with a smile on his face. He then leaned over and gave me a kiss and said, "Are you going to fix breakfast?" I said, "I am; what would you like?" He responded, "I want a real breakfast, not that bird food you like. I want some grits, sausage, eggs, toast and jelly." "OK, baby, just let me hop in the shower, and I will go downstairs and cook. Do you want some coffee while I cook, yes?" I went to take a shower, and I was going downstairs, but I was thinking still of what could be. I was so scared, and I knew he could tell. Knowing how I was raised, this was on me every day like I was a murderer. I was thinking of the love we made, and at the same time, I was scared that I was going to lose the best thing that had ever happened to me. As I finished cooking, I called him to the kitchen. We sat down and had a pleasant breakfast and started to conduct business as usual. Anthony told me that he would have everything situated as to the equipment he was going to need back in College Hill. I loved his ambition. He was simply a guy that could do whatever he desired.

Chapter 16

Conscience

That night, we had a late dinner, and I drank too much wine. I didn't know what came over me. I thought I was tripping about Jermaine coming back to our house and being near me for ten days. Anthony was discussing business over dinner and told me how important the project in Topeka was to the future of his company and our future. He said that he wanted Jermaine to become his right-hand man in Kansas and hopefully take on more responsibility as the company grew.

I was quiet and just drank wine. I had about six glasses of my favorite red Merlot. Anthony asked me why I was drinking so much tonight. That was not like me; plus, it was Thursday night. I had to work tomorrow, and I never drank more than a glass on a weeknight. I told him I was simply happy for everything that was going on for him and for us. And tonight, I wanted to celebrate. He laughed and said, "OK, do not tell me that you have a headache in the morning. Your ass is getting up if I must pull you out the bed."

I got this love. Little did he know that I was a hot mess thinking about Jermaine.

When we finally got in the bed, I was knocked out. I didn't remember even taking off my clothes. I just lay down and was out. All my thoughts, feelings and emotions were bottled up, and I could not control them. It was like a hose that had too much pressure that you knew eventually was going to explode.

What I did not think about was the cliché I was used to hearing my parents say: "A drunk mind is a sober mind." I was definitely drunk and just wanted to relax and try not to think too much. I remembered while I was sleep I was talking to my mother. We were having a sobering conversation about me, and I was confessing everything to her and asking for advice. I was telling her about how stupid I had been and that I was just an educated fool. Then out the blue, the bishop came in and was talking about the project. I was then talking about just how well we were going to do changing the entire landscape of our community. Then I saw Diane, and we were having a conversation. She was advising me to rest and relax. I then jumped up and looked around. Anthony was still asleep, but I was sweating. I was talking to myself, and I asked the Lord to please help me and protect my family. I went all off into the Lord's Prayer. I knew this is bothering me, and I knew I had to get this off my mind. I decided that I was going to tell Anthony in the morning what happened and hoped that he could forgive me.

I lay down and went back to sleep after a while only to fall back into the dream. Jermaine was here this time and was again whispering in my ear. I was getting into it, and I guessed I was loving the things he was saying. I was aroused and loving this. What a dream.

Chapter 17

Busted!!

"What the fuck you say?" Anthony was standing over me screaming. "Kevin, what the fuck did you just say?"

I was sleep, but hearing his loud voice woke me up. "What are you talking about?" I said, rubbing my head. Damn, I had a headache.

"You just said, 'Jermaine, I am liking that you got a damn hangover.' What was that? Where did that come from? Get your ass up, I want some answers."

I must have been talking in my sleep. That damn wine. Fuck!! "I don't know baby. I was drunk. I don't know what you heard or are talking about." I knew what he was talking about, but I had to play dumb. He was not hearing nothing I said. He was just screaming. "You are lying." He knew I was lying. He could always tell when I was not being truthful. It was something that he always could tell ever since we started dating as teens. For some reason, I could never lie or hide the truth from him.

He stopped screaming and looked me in my eyes. His beautiful, brown eyes were staring at my soul. I could feel them like a hot flame close to my face.

I sat up and put my head in my hands and started crying. "I am sorry, baby. I am sorry. I hope you will forgive me." "What are you talking about?" he screamed.

"Let me tell you what happened. Please calm down." He

sat on the floor and looked at me. I could not look at him, but he made me. He said to me, "Look at me and don't look away."

I looked Anthony in his eyes as he asked me to and just started to cry. It was sincere but heart-wrenching because I needed him to really understand what I was about to say. I knew he loved me as much as I loved him, but I just didn't know how to start. The only thing going through my mind was my marriage and how my husband was going to look at me. I was shamed and just did not know what to do. Anthony reached over and wiped away my tears and said to me, "Baby, what do you have to tell me?" He was just looking at me and just started to cry. I knew this was a problem because my baby never cried unless he was just upset. Before I started, I leaned over, and I give him a kiss. He said, "Baby, what is going on?" I began to talk, "Baby, back at the reunion I had a weak moment, and I was so scared to say anything." "What do you mean, you had a weak moment?" I just started to scream and sob and beg God to help me. "Anthony, please don't leave me!!" "What do you mean, leave you? Baby, what are you talking about?" Baby, when we went back to Topeka, Jermaine was flirting with me and pushing up on me extremely aggressive. It started at my parents' house and just continued. When we got to the reunion, we were decorating and meeting people. Well, I needed to take a break and went to the nurse's office to talk to the bishop. We chatted, but we chatted about opportunities coming to College Hill. We even reminisced about us growing up here in College Hill. Well, when the bishop left, I sat a little longer, and in comes Jermaine. Baby, I promise you, I didn't just do this; he came in and was very aggressive and forceful with me. He just started to kiss me, and then he pulled my pants down and started to sex me. I know it's my fault I did not tell you, but I didn't know how. Baby, I know it seems as though I was all in, but that is not true either. It was a flattering thing, but I promise you, I love you, my husband. I want my marriage with my husband. Baby, I am so sorry. I am begging you to please understand this whole thing." "Is this why you did not want him to stay at our house?" "Yes." "Did anything happen at our house?" "No." He looked at me and slapped me hard. I was really scared because I thought he was going to hit me again. I was looking at him while he chastised me. He then said, "I hired this motherfucker and made him a part of my company, and he is fucking my husband. I am so pissed right now; I do not know how to think. I am really upset because all of me was given to you, and you wanted to go back to your high school fling who had no part of our life. You helped me to change my life, and you took me for granted. I am really questioning if you really love me." My baby was really hurt; he was crying and sobbing in a way I had never seen before. He then yelled out, "Nigga, I should beat yo ass for doing this. You are playing me like a sucker." He slapped me again, and I started screaming and crying. "I don't think I would feel this way if I really didn't love you, but I need to sleep in another room. I need to find a way to forgive you and try to get through this. I cannot believe this."

I am constantly telling him, "Anthony, please don't leave. We can talk about this and make this right. I know you are mad at me, and you should be, but I know I love you and you love me. What happened is a very upsetting and hurting thing, but I will never do this again. If only you knew how I been feeling. I have been walking around here nervous and wanting to tell you what happened, but I was so afraid. I know we communicate, but I was so scared that this would happen. I am talking about this reaction I am getting from you. We have never slept apart, and we should not now. Can we please just go to sleep and talk about this in the morning?" "Kevin, shut the fuck up before I beat yo ass. I am going to the room downstairs to sleep, and you better not come down there. I am telling you, if you do, I am really going to beat yo ass. Do you understand me?" "Yes, but, baby, please, let's fix this." We always slept in the nude, but I was so turned on by his tone and dominance.

"I am going to see a therapist because I know this is not right." He walked out and slammed the door. I was sitting on the bed crying and calling his name. I was so scared that my marriage was over. I had to fix this.

Chapter 18

Morning after the Fight

After eating breakfast, he got up, got dressed and left the house. It was now 6:00 a.m.

I followed him down the stairs and begged him to talk to me because I loved him. He just jumped in his car and pulled out of the driveway.

I put on some shorts and got in my car and followed him. He was headed toward the highway, and I was right behind him. I was blowing my horn like I was crazy. He was going fast, trying to lose me.

When he pulled onto the highway, there was heavy traffic. This was the time of morning that folk were headed to work. But he was pulling in and out of traffic. Cars were blowing at him while slamming on brakes. I didn't want to lose him. I called him on my Bluetooth; it went to voice mail. I kept calling him. He picked up.

"Leave me alone, Kevin," and he hung up.

I could see his car about ten cars ahead of me. I kept trying to weave in and out of traffic. My cell rang, and when I looked down at it, *bam*, I hit the car in front of me...hard.

I was stunned as though I had been punched. I was determined to get to my husband because I knew he loved me, and I loved him. Even though I was dazed, I had to be tough. My baby told me I needed to toughen up a little. I was still thinking of him and us and knowing I had to fix this.

I just left the scene of the accident because I knew I had to get to Anthony. I felt something trickling down my face. I looked in the mirror, and I was bleeding. I was thinking I had done some real damage. It did not stop me because I was fighting for what I wanted. I was being tough like he told me, and I would not just let this happen. As I was still following him on the interstate, I could still see his car. I tried to call him one more time and got no answer. As I was looking in the sea of cars, I didn't see him anymore.

Chapter 19

Is That Anthony?

I looked out of my mirror, and I saw that there had been an accident. I called Anthony and no answer. I pulled over to make sure it was not him. Traffic was now stopped because the ambulance was trying to get all the cars in one lane. I got out of my car and started walking toward the accident. When I got close, I saw it was Anthony's car upside down and another car flipped over. There was glass everywhere. I ran over to Anthony's car, but the police stopped me. "Hold on, sir; this is a serious accident." "I am his husband," I screamed at the police. "I need to get to him now. Move the fuck out my way." I pushed the officer off me and ran toward the car. I could see Anthony still in the car upside down. The paramedics were now trying to pull him out. As they got him out the car, he was messed up. Blood was all over his face. I screamed out his name. Then I heard one of the medics say, "We are losing him..."

I was screaming and crying because it looked like the man in the other car was dead. Anthony looked like he was nonresponsive and was not responding to my voice. I was begging them to please help him. Please save him. They put him on the rolling cart and were taking him to the hospital. I got in, and I was holding his hand and praying.